T0065168

Sunshine

Dreams of Powers

JABRIL HARRIS

authorHOUSE®

AuthorHouse™
1663 Liberty Drive
Bloomington, IN 47403
www.authorhouse.com
Phone: 833-262-8899

Published by AuthorHouse 02/09/2023

ISBN: 978-1-6655-7988-9 (sc)
ISBN: 978-1-6655-7989-6 (e)

Print information available on the last page.

Any people depicted in stock imagery provided by Getty Images are models,
and such images are being used for illustrative purposes only.
Certain stock imagery © Getty Images.

This book is printed on acid-free paper.

Because of the dynamic nature of the Internet, any web addresses or links contained in
this book may have changed since publication and may no longer be valid. The views
expressed in this work are solely those of the author and do not necessarily reflect the
views of the publisher, and the publisher hereby disclaims any responsibility for them.

Contents

ACKNOWLEDGMENTS

I would like to dedicate Sunshine: Dreams of Strength to my wife, LaTonya Harris, as well as my daughters, Alyssa Colon and Autumn Harris. Tonya, I acknowledge you for believing in my dreams and encouraging me to keep writing, no matter the circumstances. I love you, and thank God for you as well. You always believed in me. To my girls, Alyssa and Autumn, thank you for inspiring my dreams to come true. You both have helped and will continue to help me grow as a father and as a man.

I will also like to acknowledge my parents, Clevon and Stacy Harris, and my brothers, Darius Hunter and Aaron Harris. Praise God for having you four in my life. To further shape and mold me through kindness, love, sacrifice, and hard work. As the days went by growing up, I was never sure at what I was good at, or what I wanted to be. Although I'm still learning, striving to be a better me is what my daily goal has become. The foundation that was set during my childhood, through my adolescence, to now as an adult, is what also led to this milestone in my life. I love you four dearly. I am proud to be your son, Dad and Mom. Darius and Aaron, I am also proud to be your brother. I hope to make you four just as proud.

To my friends and family, I would like to acknowledge you as well, for the love and support. I pray God continues to bless us through His grace and mercy. Much love and thank you again.

CHAPTER I

A Bond

Ian: Dreams are unique. They are the one thing in life that can never age. Individuals can relate to each other through dreams. Young to old. Rich to poor. Even hateful to caring. You could relive the same dream and still be in awe. Reliving your memories or living out your fantasies. Dreams can be an escape from reality that we, as people, never want to wake up from. That's what's so special about dreams. I'm sure there are countless people; who have dreamed and discover their powers, gifts, abilities, or whatever they would like to call them. That's how I discovered mine. With so many dreams, one would replay itself more than the others. Me racing away from home. I would run further and further elsewhere. Running quickly each time, too. Then, I realized, I was on route to outer space. So, believing I was running away from Earth, when actually running towards the sunlight. The very sunlight that shines bright on us. Maybe it was a metaphor of some sort. I don't know. I do know that when I reached that sun, that's when my powers came. With that dream, I would wake up stronger and faster than the time before. Every single time I had that dream, Alisha.

Alisha: The art of storytelling. Even though I've heard this story plenty of times. Seems to get better with each car ride.

Ian: Why, thank you. I don't know if you are just being nice because of the new clothes, or if you really mean it.

But I tell some of the coolest stories.

Alisha: I was just being nice, Dad (Laughing). It's definitely because of the shopping.

Ian: (Laughing) I figured. That's okay; I enjoy spending time with you. Whenever work is not in the way, I'm right here, Sunshine.

Alisha: (Smiling) You haven't called me that since my first day of kindergarten. It's nice to hear that; it makes my heart smile.

Ian: It hasn't been that long. Or has it?

Alisha: Dad, trust me. I'm going to the seventhgrade, and it has been six years since you called me that.

Ian: (Thinking) You are right. I'm sorry, Alisha, I did not know it meant that much to you. Goes to show you how fast life is passing by and missing out on what's important.

Sitting at a red light

Ian: I will do better. Alisha; I apologize for the time I've missed with you. That's on me, and I need to be held accountable for that.

Alisha: Daddy, it's okay. I know you work a lot and are always out of town. I mean, I get it; you are making a living, so I can have all the things I want. (Laughing)

Ian: (Serious, stern face) That's the thing, Alisha, all the things you require today! But tomorrow, you might just require your dad's love, support, or a hug. That's what will be most remembered. So hold me accountable for that because you are going to require it. Trust me, I know.

Alisha: Yes, sir, I will. Thank you, Daddy. (Smiling)

Ian proceeds to drive

Ian: On another note, my Sunshine will be starting the sixth grade. You will be thirteen this year. Do you know I was twelve years old when I discovered my powers? Feels like I just had the dream last night. That's how detailed that dream is for me. I will be pushing mid 30's in November. Alisha; put that in perspective. Think about your life and how you want your future to play out. That's how I know the power of dreaming.

Alisha: Why didn't you become a Dream expert? You know so much about them. (Laughing)

Ian: No patience or discipline for school. I was so used to working and helping my foster parents out. I had no time to dream anymore. So, always stay a dreamer, Alisha.

Alisha: Okay, Dad. Oh, yeah. I had a dream and might know my powers.

Ian: What? You have? When was this? Why haven't you or your Mom told me? I've been speaking about dreaming, and you didn't think to cut me off and mention that?

Alisha: Dad, you've been working. And have been talking non-stop since we've gotten to the car and the mall. And at lunch. Honestly, I forgot about it. You also have been on a business trip for the last three weeks. But The dream was two weeks ago.

Ian: Okay, my bad. You are right. Sorry for all the questions. Let's start off with this: are you excited, and was it a good dream that led to you discovering it?

Alisha: Honestly, my dream was more like a nightmare.

Ian: Interesting. (Thinking) But that's alright, Sunshine. What's most important is knowing you have some type of power. Are you scared or a little anxious, maybe eager?

Alisha: (Smiling) It was a little freighting. I don't care that much about the powers or having gifts. Especially if my friends don't have them. I want to avoid seeming like the weird kid with privileges.

Ian: Wait, you don't care? Have you not been listening to me this whole time on dreams and powers and gifts? Not everyone is gifted with powers and abilities. I'm not concerned about what your friends think. First off, no one needs to know; this is no one else's business but families. Secondly, you don't have to be proud of having any. But you have them, so don't let them go to waste. I'm serious about this.

Alisha: Sure, Dad.

Ian: Look outside your window. We are driving past diverse people and walking past hundreds throughout the day. Some with powers, some without. Some are not clear what to do with theirs, and others do not care for them. This goes back to what I was saying earlier; we are all alike but unique at the same time.

Alisha: I didn't mean like I don't care for them, and they are not necessary to have. I just don't want to be so different from anyone else or stand out for the wrong reasons. Or be looked at like a freak. No one ever noticed you had any growing up, so I don't think you would understand, Dad.

Ian: How could I not? I was a little unconventional because of this. Yes, no one knew because no one was supposed to know. But had I known then what I recognize now, that there are people like me. That would've brought me a lot more comfort. So trying not to stand out for a strange reason was hard, but I managed and made it work. I also didn't have as many friends as you do. So, what part don't I understand, Alisha? I just prefer you to be careful about what you speak about yourself, and don't worry about what others think of you. You have this gift for a reason, and hopefully, many more will come; these are blessings. Never stop dreaming, either; that's something else you don't want to lose. Understand?

Alisha: (Nodding her head) Yes, sir, I understand.

Ian: I'll have a talk with your mom, too, about keeping this away from me.

Alisha: No! You can't tell Mom I told you. It was supposed to be a surprise. I wasn't supposed to say anything, anyway. Not until dinner.

Ian: Oh, sweetheart, about that. I will not be sticking around for dinner. That was the reason for spending time with you this afternoon. I have to be at the station tomorrow morning for a meeting with Mr. Zip himself.

Alisha: So you're not staying for dinner tonight? Brian, Mom, and Erin were excited for it. Can't you hold off for your meeting?

Ian: I understand, but I need you to understand. Mr. Zip is the CEO of the company; when he wants a meeting, you meet him and can't be late or postpone. In fact, he's the one that does the rescheduling, not me.

Alisha: And?

Ian: (Chuckling) And this is my job to report to him when he asks.

Alisha: Can't you take a sick day or say you have a family emergency?

Ian: Okay, that's lying. We don't tell lies, just for the hell of it, Alisha. And most importantly, it's wrong to do.

Alisha: I get that, Dad, but would it hurt to stay just a bit longer? Please?

Ian: Alisha, I'll also be real with you; it's sometimes awkward being around them, too. Not because they're married or anything, just cause that's my ex-wife.

Alisha: We were all excited to have you over this evening. You don't have to make it so awkward with one-word sentences. Especially when mom and Brian are trying to make conversation. It's uncomfortable for them, too, I'm certain.

Ian: (Thinking) I hear what you are saying, but it's not going to change my mind on this.

Alisha: (Pouting) Even Erin was excited to have you over; she thinks you are so cool.

Ian: Erin is an exciting, happy kid; she feels everything is cool at age six

Alisha: Dad, she's seven, and she assumes you don't like her. To be honest with you, we all kind of think you don't like her.

Ian: Seven? Really? And why would I not like her? She's a child.

Alisha: You know why, Dad, because of you and Mom's divorce.

Ian: I don't blame her for our breakup. That was between your mom, Brian, and me. Your Mom, should have explained that to her already.

Alisha: She has Dad, which is why Erin feels you dislike her. She believes she is the reason that you and Mom got a divorce. That's also part of why we wanted to have you over for dinner. So, you can get to know Erin, and we can explain to her how you feel.

Ian: Brian thinks this too?

Alisha: A little, yes. He tries to play it cool, so he doesn't upset anyone, especially when Mom gets worked up.

Ian: Oh, I know how your Mom can get worked up. But sorry to disappoint, my love, but I'll speak with your mom about this and other things.

They pull into the driveway at Nicole's house. They get out of the car, and Nicole comes outside to speak with Ian.

Nicole: Hey, sweetie. How's it going, Ian? How was lunch and did you pick up some new school clothes?

Alisha: Hi, mommy! Lunch was good. And yes, can you help me with these bags?

Nicole: Brian's on his way out; he can give you a hand, and your dad too; this is a lot of clothes.

Ian: How's it going, Nicole? Lunch was good. This girl can eat.

Nicole: (laughing) I know.

Brian and Erin walked out.

Brian: Wasup Ian?

Erin: Hi Ian!

Ian: Sup, Brian. How's it going, Little E? How are you doing?

Erin: I'm good. (smiling)

Nicole: Alisha, did you ask your dad if he was staying for dinner?

Alisha: Sure did; he said no!

(Alisha hugs Ian and heads inside).

Alisha: Come on, Erin, let's play with the dollhouse. Bye, Dad. Thanks for lunch and the clothes. Love you.

Erin: Yay. I have it all set up already. Bye, Big I.

Ian: Bye. Love you too. Have fun...

Brian: Well, it would've been nice for you to stay for dinner.

Nicole: (scoffs) And why can't you stay?

Ian: Nicole, you know why. Don't act like this is brand new. I don't enjoy being around the family you've created.

Nicole: "That I've created?"

Ian: Yeah. I'm done, sugarcoating things and trying to make things work for Alisha.

Nicole: What? What are you talking about? Where is this coming from? All we asked was for you to stay for dinner.

Ian: And I said no! And when were you going to tell me that Alisha has powers?

Nicole: Oh. I see. Okay, I'm sorry about that. We were planning to inform you tonight during dinner.

Ian: We? As in, you, Brian, Alisha, and Erin? So, everyone knows except her father. This is something that I should've known right then and there. None of you can share that with Alisha. Or can relate to her with that as I can. I've never been able to experience that or share my powers with anyone until now. I just feel like a fool, not knowing she has them. And I don't want Alisha feeling the way I did growing up.

Brian: Ian, just calm down. No one was trying to upset you, trying to surprise you.

Ian: (frustrated) Brian, this is your home. I'm attempting to stay as respectful as I can. Please don't tell me to calm down. The girls are probably hearing everything we are saying still. So PLEASE, don't tell me to calm down. This happens way too often when I'm out of the loop regarding my daughter. I don't care if I'm out of town; I'm still reachable, or at least tell me to give a call back at the very least.

(Nicole glancing up at the Sun)

Brian: You seem to be getting upset; I'm just trying to defuse the situation before it escalates in front of the girls. So, what I'm saying-

Nicole: (Still watching at the Sun) Hey Brian, babe. It's ok, let's all just calm down; I'll talk to Ian, just go inside. I don't want you two going to blows. Ok, my love, it'll be fine, trust me.

Brian: Are you sure?

Nicole: Yes, my love.

Brian (walking towards the door) Okay. Hopefully, we'll see you tonight, Ian.

Ian: Yeah. Okay. (Stares at Nicole) I was going to be ok; no need to involve in that. I will not take it that far, Nicole.

Nicole:(Looks at Ian) Sure, Ian, I know you better than anyone; the Sun is pretty bright today.

Ian: (Calming down) Look, Nicole, sorry for blowing up. I just fee-

Nicole: No, I'm sorry, Ian. For everything, and I apologize for always keeping secrets from you. We can't change anything we've done in the past, but we are all trying to move forward. And this is a chance to do that. I just thought that this surprise would have made you proud, and you deserve that right now. Sorry again.

Ian: (exhales a deep breath) Okay, let's make the dinner. I'll be back. I need to get cleaned up and pick something up, at least for tonight. I can't stay long, though; I'm meeting tomorrow with Mr. Zip. And you remember how those meetings work.

Nicole: (smiling) Okay, don't be late. I'll let the girls and Brian know it's good to go. I have not forgotten, either, Ian. (Laughing) we'll have you out of here at a decent time.

Ian: Okay, see you soon.

CHAPTER 2

Dinner

(Dinner at Nicole's house. Everyone is laughing and having a good time.)

Nicole: I hope you enjoyed dinner, Ian.

Ian: I did; thank you and Brian for inviting me over. So far, so good. No arguing or even disagreements. Just a good steak with mashed potatoes and gravy. I'll have to say this has been a successful night.

Brian: I second that. Dinner was excellent, babe.

Ian: Well, Alisha. I've been dying to learn what you can do. Sorry, Nicole, she's told me that much so far.

Nicole: Maybe after dessert. We are having such a wonderful ti--

Brian: Nicole. Let's not waste his time on this. She needs to share this with her father.

Nicole: Okay. Alisha, go ahead.

Ian:, I'm ready to hear this!

Alisha: Ok, Dad. So, my abilities are somewhat complicated.

Ian: Aren't they all? (Laughing)

Nicole: Ian. (Shakes her head) Listen.

(Ian becomes confused and expresses a look of concern.)

Alisha: Dad. I think I can heal.

Ian: Okay? Cool honey. That seems like a cool-

Nicole: Ian. Let her finish.

Alisha: It might sound cool to you, Dad, but I don't like this so far-

Ian: Well, I've read stories about people restoring things, but you never know, my love. Nothing different from normal. You might cure canc-

Nicole: (getting frustrated) Ian, let her finish.

Alisha: (Dry tone of voice) Thanks, Mom. It's not like that kind of healing, Dad. I think it's just myself I can treat. I was testing it out, so I threw myself down the steps.

Ian: What?

Alisha: It didn't hurt, though, Dad; I couldn't feel a thing, and no bruise or broken bones.

Ian: Okay, now that's different, and that's so dope. Sounds like you can treat on the spot. Oh my goodness, my baby is growing up. Nicole, look at our little baby.

Nicole: IAN! Let her finish!

Ian: Damn, okay?

Alisha: I told you, Mom, I wouldn't be able to get it out, or he wouldn't understand.

Ian: I'm listening. Alisha, I'm trying to understand, sweetie.

Alisha: Daddy, this isn't cool to have. I want to try out for the cheerleading squad like the rest of my friends.

Ian: Okay, my love. You can still do that. These gifts will not hinder you from making the cheerleading squad.

Alisha: (with her head down, crying) Yes, they will, Dad. Do you not get it?

Ian: (puzzled) I'm trying to, but you still haven't told me why you wouldn't make the team.

Alisha: I would definitely make the team, but what if I don't get hurt, but should be hurt, what then?

Ian: (Even more confused) Huh, Alisha, what does that even mean? (Turns to Nicole) Can you explain, please?

Nicole: (Places her fork down) So Ian, let's say they tossed Alisha in the air, and no one catches her. She could hit the ground so hard it might cause a concussion, a broken arm, or a dislocated shoulder. That's what should take place if an accident were to happen, but for her, it wouldn't. That would cause suspicions. I'm sure you would rather not raise any auspiciousness, do you?

Ian: (Thinking, with his head down) You know I don't.

Brian: What if she went for the team but doesn't put herself in that position?

Nicole: Like how?

Brian: Maybe, She can reduce herself and her abilities. I mean, being tossed in the air is a better chance of exposure. But if she can control her outcomes, possibly that could limit the possibility of hazard.

Ian: You're a numbers guy, right, Brian?

Brian: Yes, sir, I am.

Ian: Well, wouldn't it be a higher chance of her being exposed since she's not giving the effort? Her team and coaches would notice that. Furthermore, I've been preaching about hindering yourself, which is not an option in my book.

Brian: You right didn't think of that. Any other suggestions?

Erin: (playing with her food) Maybe we could go back before she got her powers.

(All ignoring Erin except Ian)

Ian: (thinking, then smiling at Erin) That would be so cool, Erin, thank you for that.

Brian: Erin, remember, don't speak while grownups are talking. Okay.

Erin: Yes, sir.

Ian: (Sad look towards Alisha) I'm sorry, Sunshine. I know this feeling all very well. I want you to do the things that teenage girls and your friends do. This is how I sometimes felt at your age.

Alisha: Really?

Ian: Yeah, of course. Playing sports, hanging with friends, the little I had. I understand missing out because of your powers. I still believe there's a way around this, just haven't figured it out yet. If there was anything I could do right now, I would do it in a heartbeat.

(Nicole, Alisha, and Erin glance at Brian)

Ian: Everything okay? Why did they look at you like that, Brian?

Brian: Well! Maybe there is something that you can do.

Ian: Like what?

Nicole: This was the other reason for the dinner.

Brian: As you know, these gifts are somewhat like a phenomenon. People seem to have it but want to hide it, yourself included. Many don't want to be considered an outcast. Understandable for sure, but who do they talk to, or how do they seek help with either controlling these powers or hiding these powers. Take you, for instance, Ian. You have had powers since you were twelve.

Ian: Right.

Brian: Right, but you seem to be a rare case. You have an ability that no one still knows about after twenty years. On top of not having any reported incidents, you have to be a rare breed. Nicole and I of course don't have any have no abilities, but hearing Alisha talk about this, it's a struggle for her. I can only imagine what you went through keeping this bottled in. Now, we are not clear if this is based on genetics because you and Alisha share this. But did your biological parents have any? Or anyone before them have powers? Did it just start with you and now are transmitted? Were you exposed to anything, at twelve or eleven? Or even younger?

Ian: Sure, you're not an expert on this? You are asking questions I never thought to ask. I just figured I had them, and my children would too. I guess genetic is what I expected. I just would not share those thoughts either, being so secluded.

Brian: I've had to do some research to better understand you and Alisha. So, I'm trying to take this as seriously as possible. I know a little of your powers, that you somehow connect to the Sun. But I know you are a delivery driver, and I'm an accountant; it's not like we are heroes with capes, fighting for the greater good.

Ian: I hear what you are saying, Brian. I'm aware there are people like Alisha and me, living our daily lives, trying to hide this. But there's a reason we don't want the exposure.

Brian: I understand and agree. So, what if we had some guidance or someone to point us in the right direction?

Ian: Someone like whom? (concerned look) I will not ask just anyone for help. We need experts at this.

Brian: I have a brother, Will, a biology scientist. He works for a company called "DOP." This facility is thought to be helping people, with enhanced abilities, as well as researching matters like that. It's supposed to be a secret, of course, and guarded. I don't know the full details of his work because it's expected to be a secret. I'm only going off what Will has and can share with me. They, too, have the finest doctors who have specialized in therapy and tried to remove these gifts and powers. He's also been the one trying to help me with some matters regarding Alisha.

Ian: So how do they help?

Brian: Well, that, I don't know.

Ian: I've never heard of DOP. In fact, this sounds too good to be true. An organization that might be real or not, helping individuals with enhanced capabilities.

Brian: Well, this isn't for the public to know; of course, he can't tell me much. He said he works in the department that puts people asleep and sees their powers.

Ian: So why haven't you guys taken her yet? Could've had her there three weeks ago while I was on the road.

Nicole: We think you should take Alisha to see Brian's brother. Just to run some tests. He might be able to help Alisha. Cheerleading tryouts start soon, and so does school.

Ian: Still haven't said, why didn't you all take her?

Nicole: You do this type of work, and we can't just up and leave our jobs, Ian.

Alisha: Please, Dad, will you take me?

Ian: Okay, let's back up. We have another three weeks before school begins, as well as two weeks before cheer tryouts.

Alisha: Yes, so will you take me?

Ian: (looking at Brian and Nicole) Whose insurance would this be on? How much will this cost?

Nicole: All of that, and you are worried about coverage? Really, Ian?

Ian: Hell yeah, this sounds like some expensive visits. There's a reason I'm asking.

Brian: Ian, my brother has already said it's for free.

Ian: You all have already spoken with him on this. What the Hell, Nicole? What if this gets out to the press or social media? Alisha's life would be ruined. And there would be horrible people lined up at your door after our daughter.

Alisha and Erin's eyes widened.

Brian: Trust me, Ian, we know! That's why my brother hasn't said anything.

Nicole: Has Alisha told you about the whole extent of her dream?

Ian: No!

Alisha: I didn't get the chance to. Dad talked a lot.

Ian: What's the whole extent?

Erin: Mommy, I'm scared. I don't want to hear this Dream again.

Alisha: And I don't like even thinking about it, let alone talk about it.

Nicole: I understand; this is an uncomfortable and scary thing to discuss. Alisha, we'll talk more with your dad about this if you'd like? You can take Erin upstairs to watch some TV. I'll bring dessert up to you both soon.

Alisha: Okay, Mom.

Ian: I'll see you in a bit, Honey.

Nicole: Ian, I need you to remain calm. Ok? When I tell you this.

Ian: Don't tell me to remain calm, Nicole; you know I hate that. Just tell me what else is going on. Please.

Nicole: Ian, you are like an expert at dreams; you understand dreams better than anyone I've ever known.

Ian: Like I've told Alisha, I'm not an expert, far from it. I can remember my dreams a lot better than others. I just try to explain your dreams and what they mean, but that doesn't mean I'm a professional. I had to do my research on dreams. That's the only thing I felt I needed to survive.

Brian: We get that, Ian. But how dangerous or real can a dream become?

Ian: From what I've read, experienced, and told Nicole in the past. Dreams can somewhat be like visions. That has some meaning to them. They could represent something or foreshadow, too. For Alisha and I foreshadowed our abilities. The other thing about dreams is controlling them, or as they call them today, lucid dreams. I've met no one who can do this. I for certain can't do it, and I'm pretty positive Alisha can't either. So, I'll ask again what happened in Alisha's dream. (Ian becoming frustrated)

Nicole: So Alisha is running on these peaks. Why was she in the mountains? Your guess is as good as ours. Then, she's attacked by a shadowy figure. She said that the figure grabbed her but couldn't hold on to her. So, Alisha runs away. As she's running, she sees people on the other side of her. Some old and others were as young as Erin's age. But they are getting consumed by this shadowy figure. The figure becomes faster and catches up to Alisha, by the time she gets to the top of the mountain. As she's about to be taken, she jumps from the top of the mountain, only to be awakened, falling down the steps. She was sleepwalking this whole time, too, Ian.

Ian: So, this shadowy character. Is it him, Nicole?

Nicole: I'm not certain?

Ian: Stop with the lies, Nicole! Is it him?

Brian: From what Nicole has told me about your past, Ian, it is.

Ian: Thank you, Brian! Dammit, y'all should've said something a lot sooner. I would have been back earlier from the business meeting. Mr. Zip would have understood. We are way behind and at a disadvantage.

Nicole: What difference would that have made? It's still him, and it's a matter of time before he finds her.

Ian: The earlier I could've known, the faster this could've been resolved.

Nicole: How? You haven't seen him in nineteen years. You've actually never seen him, come to think of it.

Ian: I also didn't have the powers, the strength, or knowledge then either. Not being able to recognize him would not have been the problem.

Brian: If he's been around since we were kids, why isn't he dead by now?

Ian: I don't know, Brian. But I know the dream world and our physical world or let's just say reality, work differently, especially dealing with time.

Brian: There are no reports or articles on this guy.

Ian: Why would there be? Some people just wouldn't believe it, anyway. I know just some things about him, and how I got off his radar. It took a while, but I had to sacrifice sleep.

Nicole: So she can't sleep, c'mon Ian. The girl has to sleep; you just feel, "she'll be wasting productive time" sleeping.

Ian: What? That's not the reason.

Brian: Let's calm down.

Ian: Brian, please don't say that.

Nicole: No, let's get real here for a second, Ian. When you explained him to me twelve years ago, he doesn't sound that scary. And Alisha could just be a little shaken up.

Ian: You weren't there, Nicole! You don't know how his presence felt. I was twelve and terrified, just like Alisha.

Brian: I'm more worried about Alisha, but Ian, he didn't sound as intimidating as you might imagine now.

Ian: I'm going to stop you both right there. This is the exact reason I didn't tell anyone. I was too afraid that no one would be with me on this. Let me ask you something, Brian. Has Nicole described who he is?

Brian: She's spoken enough: a man who's in your dreams trying to take your powers. That's how you discover what you have.

Ian: That's all she's told you, huh?

Brian: Yeah.

Ian: Did she also say that each time you go to sleep, the chances that he can track your physical body increase?

Brian: No.

Ian: Or how about his goons, searching for you? Neighbor to neighbor? Door to door? There is no hiding in your dreams or real world?

Brian: No!

Ian: How, once he has your powers, he kills you and anyone else that disrupts his goals? He's pure evil.

Brian: I didn't know all of this. I'm sorry, Ian. Seems like I wasn't told the whole truth, either.

Nicole: Great, now that we're all caught up, we need to start moving.

Ian: And Brian, did she mention you cannot sleep longer than an hour? Time moves differently in the Dreamworld, as I've stated before. He has a lot more control once he meets you. You need to sleep in increments to keep him guessing, and, he won't be able to locate you.

Nicole: We get it, Ian! Damn, I'm a horrible person who's underestimated the hype or physical myth.

Ian: It is not about you, Nicole. I couldn't care less what you think. Stop doing that?

Nicole: Doing what, Ian?

Ian: (Yells) Making it about you! This isn't about what you think. Our daughter has the same fear I had; that should be enough. Not because of cheerleading or because you just want this to go away. But because this is real, our daughter can have some type of long-suffering from this, just as I did.

Brian: Hey! Can you two put this aside right now, so we can figure this out? I'm getting worried.

Ian: Brian, you should be disturbed. When the dreams began to happen, he killed my parents looking for me. I thought they abandoned me, hadn't seen them or heard from them for years. Until I found out the truth. The Dream Man killed them! I couldn't sleep for months.

Brian: Dream Man?

Ian: Yes, I never got his name, so that's what I came up with to call him.

Brian: He killed your parents? Damn, is this also the reason you grew up in foster care?

Ian: Yeah. He's the reason I bounced around after he murdered them trying to get to me. Then killed my first foster parents too. He caused all the loneliness until I met Nicole.

Brian: Damn, sorry to hear that, Ian. I had no clue. I'm sorry, I just doubted you. Nicole never told me any of this.

Nicole: It was something we never talked about, even when we were married. Seemed to bring him a lot of pain.

Ian: It sometimes did, but it doesn't too much now.

Brian: I think we owe you a sincere apology, Ian.

Ian: No need, all is well. I just feel the sooner I could've known, the faster this could've been resolved.

Brian: How powerful do you think he is?

Ian: Was? I don't know.

Brian: No, I mean, how powerful do you think he is? Alisha said his force almost felt like a magnet being attached to her.

Ian: I'm not sure about him, but I also don't care. I didn't have the fearless thought process I have now. Powers or no powers, I'm protecting my daughter at all costs and will take him down if he wants war.

Brian: This is wild. I never imagined I'll be talking about dreams and powers and a serial dream killer.

Ian: How long ago did she dream this? I need a date and time too.

Nicole: The week you went on your business trip at 3:48 in the morning. Thursday, July second.

Ian: Ok, have you guys stayed in contact with Brian's brother?

Brian: Like we said, we mentioned it to him, and he just asked us to get back with him. I did not know the severity of this dude and dreams and everything else. Don't know what to make of this. What else should we have informed him?

Nicole: His brother also never asked Ian.

Ian: You guys should have kept him updated on her. Sleep schedule. Her reactions.

Brian: Ok, slow down. This is becoming very heavy, and we'll be moving too fast on this.

Ian: We have to be, Brian. We need to be very aggressive from here on out. No more mistakes or secrets. Has Alisha talked to or been in contact with any of her friends? These are the things that you should take notes of because Dream Man has been collecting notes on Alisha.

Nicole: Of course, she's been in contact with them.

Ian: Ok, we need to let their parents know about the whole sleep scheduling too. I don't care about cheerleading practice or if we are outcasts. This is about life or death. And it's not fair to let people, innocent people die or be harmed, especially when they have no clue on what's going on. Have there also been kids dying or being hurt, Brian? Since you stay up with the news and social media.

Brian:, I have been so focused on powers and things. I have not been able to keep up with any of that. Even work has taken the back burner to this.

Ian: Okay. The last thing I need to know is, did he say anything to her or speak at all in her dream?

Nicole: She did say that he yelled out, "No!" Very aggressive and angry.

Ian thinking

Nicole: Ian? What do you think?

Ian still thinking

Nicole: Ian? Say something!

Ian: It has to be him.

Brian: Do you think his crew has powers too?

Ian: Not sure; we'll find that out too.

Nicole: So this sleep schedule, how do we know this works?

Ian: When I told my foster parents, they had me sleeping in hour increments. So, I would sleep for an hour around midnight, then stay up until I would go to school. At school, I would sleep during lunch, since lunch was just thirty minutes long. Then sleep no more than an hour when I got out of school and got home. And would do this cycle all over again until my foster parents felt that I was safe.

Brian: They never reached help for you? I mean, my brother has been doing this for a while; someone had to be helping people with powers out.

Ian: Times are different now. They wouldn't have been able to afford it. So, I was very sleep-deprived for most of my teen years. That's the reason I get little rest to this day.

Brian: I've learned more about you tonight, Ian, than in the past 5 years.

Ian: (chuckles) My wife slept with you, Brian, cheated on me and had another child outside our marriage. I'm still trying to forgive her and you for that. It wasn't easy coming over here, and it hadn't been easy to hold a conversation with someone who I feel stole my family. But I'm learning to forgive you both and forgive myself for that hate I have.

Nicole: What I did was wrong, Ian. I've apologized and acknowledged that Brian and I both have.

Ian: I know, and I think tonight was needed. Sorry for getting upset earlier. I just want the best for our daughter and will stop at nothing to gain that. But we have to move fast now. Agreed?

Brian and Nicole both agree with a head nod

Ian: Look, they've been on their way and have had three weeks to get all the information they require. I need to get home and pack a few bags. Also, give Mr. Zip a call to let him know I won't make it in tomorrow for the meeting. Have Alisha's bags packed and ready to go. I'll be back.

Alisha: MOM, Dad! (Running down the stairs with Erin) I think someone is in the backyard!

(There's a knock on the door. They begin to all look at each other)

Ian: They're here!

Chapter 3

Nightcap

(Another knock on the door)

Police: Hello! Is anyone home? This is the Arch West Police Department.

Brian: (Opens his phone to look at the cameras) There's definitely someone back there. (Whispering) Also, two officers are in the front.

Nicole: The one in the back, is he dressed like an officer too? (She whispers)

Brian: I can't tell; I would imagine so.

Ian: Have you all had the police show up before?

Brian: Not at all.

Ian: Really?

Brian: Yes, really; what is that supposed to mean?

Ian: It's not too many brothers out here in this neighborhood. You might want to be careful answering that door. In fact, I don't think this is the police at all, to be honest with you.

Nicole: I'm getting that feeling too. Girls go back upstairs.

Erin: Mommy, I want to stay with you. I'm scared.

Brian: Erin, do as your mother asks of you. Alisha, can you take your sister back upstairs, please?

Nicole: I would feel safe with them staying with us.

Ian: No, he's right, Nicole. This might get ugly.

Brian: Ugly, how? I'm not about to fight some cops.

Officer: (Knocking again) We hear you talking in there. We just want to do our job, and end our shift. Please answer the door.

Ian: I'll go to the back and deal with him; let me get your phone.

Brian: Deal with him how? Are you going to speak with him? I'm sure he's back to being safe.

Ian: Brian. Trust me on this. These are not cops. (Turns to Alisha and Erin) Alisha, go upstairs and hide in the closet or underneath the bed. I don't want you or Erin to come out until we say so. Understand?

(Alisha and Erin have a concerned look.)

Alisha: What are you about to do? Do you think it's him? Do you think he found us? Mom, I haven't seen this; I don't know what to do.

Ian: Alisha, don't panic. Stay calm. It will be ok. (whispers in her ear) Be strong for Erin. She will need it right now. Okay, Sunshine?

Alisha: (takes a deep breath) Yes, sir. (Turns to Erin) C'mon, Erin, let's play hide and seek from the cops. They can't hurt us if they can't find us, all right?

Erin: (Tearfully) Yes.

Alisha: Ok, let's go hide then.

Ian: Ok, Brian, answer the door and stall them. Get out of the way when I say move.

Brian: Man, don't get us hurt or killed in my home, Ian.

Ian: Trust me, Brian.

Nicole: Brian, he knows what he's doing; we will be fine.

Ian: Nicole, come with me to the back. And grab Brian's phone.

Ian and Nicole head to the back, and Brian jogs to the front door

Brian: (Yells) I am on my way, sorry! (Opens the door) Hello officers, what seems to be the problem?

Officer 1: Good evening, sir, AWPD. Got a complaint from some neighbors that there were loud, disruptive noises coming from your home, is everything okay this evening?

Brian: Yes, sir, just having dinner with the wife and kids.

Officer 1: (smiling) We just want to make sure everything's okay. Kind of figured that was the case, mister...?

Brian: Bost, Brian Bost.

Officer 1: Okay, Mr. Bost, can we spea-

Brian: You know what, I'm positive it was the Smiths that called in. Always in someone's business.

Officer 1: Not sure who call-

Brian: They might've heard us playing UNO, that game gets pretty intense. Family or not, I'm trying to win. We gone bust out the Spades cards in a minute too. To see who can hang with this family or not. Know what I'm saying? (obnoxious laugh)

Officer 1: I'm afraid not, sir. Can we speak with your wife Mr. Bost.

Brian: Umm, sure thing. (yells) Babe, Nicole? Could you come here, please?

Meanwhile, at the back of the house while Brian stalls

Ian: (whispering)Do you see him still?

Nicole: (Looking at the camera on Brian's phone.) Yeah, I see him. He's not in uniform, though.

Ian: (whispering) I figured these guys weren't cops. Where exactly is he at?

Nicole:(whispering) He's waiting behind the door or on the side of the door. More to our left.

Ian: (whispering) Ok, does he look like he's about to open it?

Brian calls for Nicole in the background

Nicole: (whispering)No, it seems like he's waiting for something.

Ian: (whispering) Or someone. Ok, I'm good now; I'll deal with him. Go back up there and stall with Brian. Say you were putting the kids to bed. And cut the front light out.

Nicole: (whispers back) What, why? They'll probably want to speak with them. When would I cut the lights?

Ian: (whispering) Damn, Nicole, just do it and trust me on this. You'll know when to cut it off.

Nicole: (whispering) Okay. Ian, don't take too much time.

Brian: (In the background, still by the front door) Nicole?

Ian: (whispering) Like I said, trust me. I got this.

Nicole: (Whispering) This better work. Don't get my babies hurt, Ian.

Ian: I won't!

Nicole steps away from Ian and gets to the hallway

Nicole: Here I come (shuffling like she's in a rush). Yes, my love. Oh, hi, Officers.

Officer 1: Evening, Mrs. Bost. We're sorry to bother you. We have a couple of complaints. Everything okay?

Nicole. Oh, why yes. All good tonight, having a nightcap with the husband. You know, I might've gotten a little loud after a few bottles of wine. Played some UNO. And was practicing some routines with my daughter. Trying out for the cheerleading team.

Officer 1: Understandable. (Looks at Ian's truck.) Have a friend over too?

Brian: Oh yes, the ex. He just got back in town to visit our daughter.

Officer 2: Where are they?

Nicole: Just put the youngest to bed. That's what took me a while to come to the door.

Officer 2: Where's your husband and oldest at?

Nicole: In the kitchen.

The officers look at one another, and the second officer goes to contact the third in the back. Ian Has his ear to the side of the door, waiting for officer 3 to move. He hears officer 3's radio.

Officer 2: (through radio) They're separated, clear to get her.

Officer 3: (radios back) Copy.

Officer 2: Can we speak with your ex-husband and your oldest, Mrs. Bost?

Nicole: Umm, that's okay. Everyone is good; we'd just like to get back to our night.

Officer 1: I think it's best we step inside.

Brian: No, thanks. But appreciate you stopping by. (trying to shut the door) Goodnight.

Officer: (stops Brian from shutting the door) I'm afraid I'll need to speak with the guest and your kids.

While in the back, Ian hears the back door creek open.

Ian Let's the Officer get halfway in, BAM! Ian smashes Officer 3's head into the backdoor. Officer 3 unprepared, is now dazed. Ian then grabs and holds onto Officer 3's collars. Ian drops to the ground, falling backward, kicks his right leg up, and tosses Officer 3 into the backyard. Officer 3 realizes what's happening after the toss and hitting the ground.

Officer 3:(While on the ground, rolls over to his belly, puts his hand out to plead) Wait. Wait!

Ignoring the officer's plea, Ian Runs towards him, and soccer kicks him in the face. Knocking Officer 3 out cold. Ian checks for any weapons and grabs his gun from his waist. Officer 3 regaining his conscious, he sees Ian standing over top of him.

Officer 3: (Still dazed) Hey what are, what are you doing?

Ian: (whispering) Who are you? What are you here for?

Officer 3: The girl. He wants the girl.

Ian: He who? I need a name.

Officer 3: No. (pulls a blade from his sleeve and tries to stab Ian from the side)

Ian: (sees the knife in his peripheral, counters the knife attack.) Then I'm sorry. (Takes the knife and stabs Officer 3 in the chest.)

(Back to the front door)

Officer 1: Look, we have been patient; get your ex and your daughter to this door.

(Nicole sees Ian behind the second officer. She cuts the light out)

Officer 2: Ma'am, turn that light back on pleas-

Ian snaps Officer 2's neck and pushes Officer 2's body into Officer number 1 into the house.

Brian: (Loudly) WOAH!

Nicole and Brian both fall backward in the house

Nicole: Ahh!

Officer 1: Who the hell-

Ian: Shut up. (Ian tells the police. Ian pulls a gun out toward the officer. Then Ian kicks the officer onto his back.) Nicole, can you get up, close, and lock the door? For us.

Nicole: (Stands up and walks towards the door.) Sure can.

Ian: Brian, get his gun out of his holster.

Brian: (Confused) Ian, what the hell are you doing? Are you crazy?

Ian: Not as crazy as I will be if you don't grab this fool's gun.

Officer 1: This will not end well for you; you need to let me go.

Ian: (Takes the butt of the gun and hits the officer.) Shut up, and I won't say it again?

Officer 1: Ahh!

Brian: (In shock) What the Hell? Ian? Why would you--

Ian: No time for all this, Brian; I'll answer your questions just as soon as this fake cop answers my questions.

Nicole: Brian, come sit down, sweetie, let him work.

Alisha is chasing after Erin. Erin's heading downstairs.

Ian: Stop them; I don't want them to see this.

Alisha, screams, while Erin runs towards Brian crying.

Alisha: OMG, is he dead? Mom? Is he dead?

Erin: (crying) What is wrong with his neck?

Ian:(Frustrated) Take them back upstairs, please!

Nicole: (Grabs Alisha and Erin) I told you two to stay upstairs. Get back up there. Erin, close your eyes.

Ian: (Leans in closer towards the officer) Did "HE" send you?

Officer: Who is "HE" (laughing)

Ian: (Takes the butt of the gun and hits the officer again) You know who I'm talking about. I will not waste time with you. Best tell me who "HE" is now, and I might spare your life for coming here for our daughter.

Brian: (Scared, cracked voice) Oh my goodness, Ian, this is bad. He doesn't know who you're talking about. This is a big mist-

Officer: He will be here soon (widen eyes). You don't have to spare my life. He will kill me for even telling you that (laughing) I'm already dead. No escaping from him. Don't go to sleep!

Ian: (Grabs a sofa pillow) Thanks for the advice. (Shoots and kills the officer.)

Ian walks towards the back door to grab officer 3 from the backyard.

Brian: (In disbelief) What the hell just happened?

Nicole walks back into the living room.

Nicole: A lot just happened. I know, my love, let's just stay calm.

Brian: Calm? We all just watched Ian fight, interrogate, then execute a man. Cops on top of it all.

Ian drags officer 3 into the house, then lays him on top of officer 2.

Ian: They're not cops, Brian.

Brian: Sure, let's drag another body in here. Blood on the floor. Sofa pillow with a bullet hole through it.

Nicole: What now, Ian?

Ian: I'll be back. To help clean this up.

Brian: You'll be back to clean this up? Are you serious? We have three dead cops in this house. Where did you learn that from? I mean, you did that effortlessly. And have no type of emotion behind it. I mean, 15 minutes ago, we were just talking about a loving family. What the hell just happened?

Ian: First off, they're not cops. They're with the Dream Man. See! (shows fake badges.) Secondly, I was taught to do that.

Brian: When? The last three weeks on a business trip?

Ian: No, about twelve years ago. That's what I do for a living.

Brian: A trained killer. I thought you were a recruiter. Or delivery driver, courier, or whatever it is you do!

Ian: I am a recruiter, was a delivery driver. It's a complicated position I have. I'm still a courier, just not your typical courier anymore. And haven't been for years.

Brian: Clearly! You have been around a trained killer all these years. Nicole, why aren't you freaking out?

Nicole:(Looking at the bloodstain on the floor) I wonder how I can get that out of the floor and carpet. So, Ian, now what?

Brian: Wait, you knew about this, Nicole?

Nicole: Of course, we were married for six years, Brian.

Ian: Look, Brian. Can you ask questions, and help at the same time? We are on a tight schedule now.

Brian: Tight schedule? This isn't normal!

Nicole: Brian, honey. I'll fill you in later. Right now, we need to get moving. We have little time.

Brian: We can do the filling in now. These are massive gaps that need to be explained.

Ian: Brian, settle down and stay focused.

Brian: Don't tell me to settle down, please. I'm freaking out over here. This is crazy; what do you do for a living, Ian.

Ian: Ok, Brian. To summarize, You know I work with Zip, the delivery company. I delivered packages for Zip for about a year, then got in good with the owner, Mr. Zip. He began to run a side business, one that my powers would be more of useful. Since then, and I've been the companies muscle, brain, and power source. You might look at as mercenary employment, because of the money. But, my work is necessary and helpful in the long run. I go to different cities, states, or even countries to help those in need of saving. Only for the right price, though, too. No jobs ever for free. Mr. Zip and I have been using these powers or trying to use these powers for the better or greater good.

Brian: (Overwhelmed, takes a seat on the couch) What? So you are not a recruiter?

Ian: Occasionally, I am sent to track those with special powers. To help them, not to hurt them though.

Brian: Where did you learn all this from?

Ian: I have been trained by the world's greatest in almost all categories. So most fighting styles I've mastered. I'm a great shot too. I can interrogate and, negotiate to the highest degree. All that to do my work excellently and be the most professional. I am the best at what I do, very reliable to the company Zip, and very valuable and profitable for Mr. Zip himself. It might not be the most honorable, morally, or ethical job to most. But it's very rewarding financially, and saving those in need or danger keeps me going back. Especially when it comes to being this special courier, I feel I'm giving my best to society. Any more questions?

Brian: Actually, no. You just explained that very well. I might not agree with it, but I know tonight it just saved our lives. So thank you, and no judgment here. Sorry for all the questions, Ian.

Ian: Thank you. I'll get rid of the bodies and get Alisha to your brother. If he's not too far, we can get this done tonight.

Brian and Nicole look at each other.

Brian: About that.

Ian: What? Let me guess, the facility is closed tonight?

Brian: It's not that. My brother is staying in Minnesota. The facility is in Saint Cloud, Minnesota.

Ian: What? Minnesota? Why wasn't this mentioned at first?

Nicole: We knew this would be your reaction. So, are you going to do it or not?

Ian: I've already agreed to it, and it's for my Alisha. Just have her bags packed when I return. I need to run home and pack some bags real fast, too. I have to call Mr. Zip to let him know this situation, and somewhere I can bury these bodies. Just need help putting them in my truck. Do you mind, Brian?

Brian: Not at all. What can Mr. Zip do for you? Do you want him involved in this?

Ian: Yes, he knows a thing or two about someone trying to kill you, them failing, and him covering it up.

Ian and Brian get the bodies in the bed of his truck. The next-door neighbor, Mr. Smith, is outside.

Brian: (quietly says) Oh great.

Ian: (whispers) What?

Brian: (whispering) Nosey ass Smith is out here on his porch.

Ian: (whispering) Ok, play it cool, you got this.

Smith: Evening, fellas.

Brian: Wasup Smith, how's your night going?

Ian: Wasup, man.

Smith: Night's going good. Need some help there? Looks pretty heavy.

Brian: Nah, we're good, thanks.

Smith: Sounds like a lot of noise over there started to call the cops to make sure everything's alright (laughing)

Brian: (sarcastically laughs) Aw Smith, man, you are hilarious.

Ian and Brian throw the last body in the truck.

Smith: (waves him off, still chuckling) I get that a lot.

Brian: Alright now, Smith, let me get back to my folks

Smith: Ok, now have a goodnight (watching them go back inside)

Alisha comes back downstairs.

Alisha: (has her left hand blocking the view of the dead bodies.) Daddy.

Ian: Alisha, I'll be back.

Nicole: Where is your sister?

Alisha: Sleeping. I set the alarm; I'm going to bed too, just overheard everything Dad said.

Ian: Alisha. I didn't want you to know this part of my life at all. (head down)

Alisha: No matter what, Dad. I love you, and thank you for tonight.

Ian: (lifts his head and smiles) Anything to keep you safe. Remember Nicole, only an hour. Then she wakes back up. I shouldn't be gone that long.

Nicole: Okay. See you soon.

As Ian leaves out and closes the door behind him, he hears Nicole ask Alisha.

Nicole: Did you see any of this play out like this?

Alisha: No Ma'am, I didn't.

CHAPTER 4

Road Trip

It's now morning. Ian has returned to pick Alisha up.

Brian: Wasup Ian?

Ian: What's going on, Brian? How are you feeling?

Brian: Little traumatized. I saw three dead bodies in my home last night and watched my wife and her ex-husband act like it's the norm.

Nicole: Whatever, Brian. Ian, he hasn't stopped talking about last night.

Ian: Morning, Nicole. And sorry about that, Brian. Just trying to keep you all safe.

Brian: Oh no, thank you! I learned not to pick a fight with you, too. You'll have to teach me a few of those moves.

Ian: Sure thing. (Chuckling)

Brian: (Whispering) Hey, where did you put the bodies?

Nicole: Why are you whispering?

Brian: Shhh.(whispering) keep it down, didn't want the girls knowing Ian caught a few bodies. They might get scared of him. Hell, I am a bit now after last night.

Nicole: Ugh, Goodness.

Ian: (Whispering) Hey Brian, if I told you, I would have to show. And you know how that can be right, man. Let's keep it low-key.

Brian: Right, keep it discreet. Smart.

Ian: Also, it's not safe for you three to be here. You guys can follow us to a safe house in Iowa if you'd like.

Nicole: No need, we're heading to my parents.

Brian: Wait? A safe house? I don't know, babe; that sounds a bit more "discreet," don't you think?

Nicole: No, not really. We'll be fine over at my parents, Ian. Thanks, though.

Ian: Okay, how have your parents been, anyway?

Nicole: Good, they ask about you all the time. They wish you would drop by more often to catch up. I tell them you are a busy man nowadays.

Ian: I guess I'll have to. I miss them too.

(Alisha walks downstairs, texting someone, dragging her bags.)

Alisha: Hi Daddy!

Ian: Morning, baby. Do you need all these bags? We will only be gone for a few days, my love. Stop dragging the bags, too; that's how you mess them up.

Alisha: Well, I have a few heavy things in here.

Ian: (stops Alisha and opens up her bag) Why do you need a brick? And leave that phone.

Alisha: Daddy? Why do I need to leave the phone? And yes, I might need to switch outfits all these bags to keep our identity safe. We never know who's watching us. This brick might also save our lives later. You never know.

Ian: Okay, well, we don't need anyone tracking your phone or tracking us, for that matter. In fact, Nicole, you have to break the phone and throw it out. This isn't a spy movie, baby. It does not work like that. (smiling) Okay, my love.

Alisha: Okay.

Ian: We have to get going. Before anyone else gets here. Okay? So say goodbye and go wait in the car for me.

Alisha: Okay. Bye, Mom. I love you. Love you too, Brian. I'll see you soon.

Ian: Make sure to tell your sister too.

(Erin walks downstairs with a bag too.)

Erin: Actually, Mr. I, Mommy said I could come too.

Ian: What? No, no, no, little E. You need to stay here with your mommy and daddy. This isn't a road trip, sweetie, and we don't have time to discuss this either. Right, Mommy and Daddy?

Brian: Hey Alisha, can you take your sister outside while we speak with your Dad?

Alisha: Sure thing!

(Alisha and Erin walk outside and head towards the car.)

Ian: What the Hell! Why would you guys tell her to come along? This will get dangerous!

Nicole: That's exactly why. More people might show up back around, and they are already tracking Alisha. What if they come back for leverage? Then not only are we in danger, but so is Erin.

Ian: She's not my responsibility. She will more than likely get in the way too. And if something happens to her, I don't want that on my conscience. She needs to stay here.

Brian: Ian, she had a dream last night.

Ian: ... Yeah? Ok?

Brian: More like a nightmare of a man trying to hurt her. That's what she told us this morning.

Ian: (Takes a deep breath) What are her powers?

Nicole: We don't know. She doesn't know. She might not have any. It could just be the Dream Man after her. To get to Alisha.

Brian:, Please? I already told my brother, and we were going to ask, so she could get that test run too. Just in case they come back.

Ian: Okay, but if anything happens to her... I'll let you know, but it will be on your hands, not mine. I'll still protect her, but my main focus is Alisha, understood?

Nicole: Okay.

Brian: Thank you, Ian.

Ian: I'll talk to her in the car to better describe him. You should say a real goodbye, just in case. Hate speaking this way, but there's always a possibility that... (pauses) I'll be waiting in the car.

(Ian starts the car, backs out of the driveway, and they all wave goodbye as they're heading down the street. Ian tells them the directions he's taking to Minnesota.)

Ian: Ok, so this is a serious task we are doing. We need to make to Minnesota today, and it takes about seven to nine hours to get there from here. We will go through the city of St. Louis, which goes from Highway 270 to Highway 70.

(Alisha and Erin just look at each other, confused.)

Alisha: Is that going east?

Ian: No, that's going west. Keep up. Write this down if need be.

Erin: Let me get my Paw Patrol notebook. One second... Ok, I'm ready.

Ian: Next we will go through Highway 61 NORTH (Ian turns to Alisha.) which takes us north of 27 just outside of Davenport. We will stop for food and a bathroom break at that time. Still with me, girls?

Alisha and Erin nodded their heads yes.

Ian: Cool, then we will continue on from Highway 27 north until we reach Highway 35 north; from there, we should be in Minnesota. I'll find a phone and contact your uncle, to get the exact directions to the facility.

Alisha: You lost me going to St. Louis.

Erin: Will we get to pass by the Arch?

Ian: Just go for the ride Alisha; pay attention too; you might need this someday.

Alisha: Sure, Dad.

Erin: So, can we stop at the Arch?

Ian: No, Little E, we have to get you to safety. We want to stay ahead of schedule and ahead of them. Okay?

Erin: (Sadly) Okay.

Ian: It's also supposed to be cloudy and possibly rain, so we need to get there asap.

Erin: What is asap

Ian: As soon as possible. We will also have twenty minutes of quiet time each hour.

Erin: I love the quiet game; I can stay quiet longer than anyone else.

Ian: (whispers to himself) I certainly hope so.

Alisha: And what do we do when we are not sleeping?

Ian: Ahh, you too can color. I have a few coloring books.

Erin: Yay.

Alisha: Color?

Ian: Play I Spy.

Erin: One of my favorite games, I spy.

Ian: Mine's too, Erin. You got dolls, right? Or patty cake when the quiet game isn't being played.

Alisha: Daddy, this will be a boring ride. Why couldn't I bring my phone?

Ian: Alisha, I told you already why. They can track us. No electronics at all, no cellphones, Video games, or tablets. Look outside and see the scenery too.

Alisha: UGH! This will be boring.

Ian: Watch it, Alisha! (stern look towards Alisha)

Erin: (chuckling)

Alisha: (rolling her eyes at them both and folding her arms) well, I'll take my hour nap now, I guess.

Ian: Okay, do that then. I'll be timing you; it starts when I hear the first snore. You know Alisha snores loud, doesn't she, Erin.

Erin: (laughing) Yeah, she does!

Ian: (Laughing) You should try to get some rest too, Little E. I will wake you up at 9:48. Okay?

Erin: Okay.

Ian: I'll play a CD to help you sleep. Alisha used to fall asleep to this all the time at your age.

Erin: What is it?

Ian: Just nursery stories. Get some rest.

Erin: No. what's a CD?

Ian: You don't know what a CD is? Never mind that. Just listen and get some rest.

Erin: (yawning) Ok, Big I.

(One hour later.)

Ian: Girls, time to wake up. Alisha. Erin. Time to wake up. C'mon, girls, rise, and shine.

Alisha: Just a few more minutes (vaguely saying)

Ian: Nah, girls, time to wake up. For real, come on now.

Alisha: Okay. Daddy, I'm woke, I'm woke.

Ian: Did you get some sleep, my love? Or not enough?

Alisha: (Grumpy) Not nearly enough. When's the next time we can sleep? It won't be until after we get some lunch. Erin, you woke back there?

Erin: I'm still sleepy.

Ian: (chuckles) I know, and I'm sorry, girls. But you can't sleep longer than an hour. We have already discussed this. I understand the frustration, trust me. But there's a formula to this, so the Dream Man can't track you.

Alisha: Yeah, we know, Dad; where are we anyway now?

Ian: (Begins to read the road map out load.) Okay, so we are passing through Vandalia and Bowling Green. This is right outside of St. Louis.

Alisha: Why didn't you just GPS it, Dad? So, we can all see where we are at.

Ian: I told you no electronics. This goes for me as well. I can't tell you; the children to do something, and I do the opposite. That's called hypocrisy.

Erin: Hyposify?

Ian: Hypocrisy. Or being a hypocrite. That means if you are teaching or telling someone something but not doing it yourself. So, if I'm telling you, Erin or your sister Alisha don't lie to me or don't get on any electronics; but I go and lie to you or Alisha, or get on my cellphone. That's being a hypocrite. Do you understand?

Erin: I think so.

Ian: Always remember, Erin, to practice what you preach. Always do the right thing, even if it means getting into trouble or someone might get their feelings hurt. That's what you call character, or having good character.

Erin: Okay. So, is that why you beat up those bad men? Is that why we are going to see Uncle Will? Weren't they good characters? Were they hypofits?

Ian: (disturbed) Um, lots of questions there. I don't think we should discuss what happened to those men last night. Just know the bad men didn't get to you or your sister. You shouldn't have seen that last night either; you were supposed to be under the bed anyway, playing hide and seek with Alisha.

Alisha: Dad, we heard everything. We couldn't help but look to see what was going on. Erin and I watched you kill one in the backyard first.

Erin: Yeah, it was really scary.

Ian: We'll let's not talk about it anymore. Just forget what you saw last night in the backyard.

Alisha: Okay. (pausing) so what about the cops in the living room?

Ian: What about them? They weren't real cops. And once again, get off the subject, Alisha.

Erin: Yep, one cop's neck was really twisted!

Ian: Okay, get that image out of your head, Erin. This is not a conversation we're having!

Alisha: Dad? We are just askin-

Ian: Drop it, not another word!

Erin: So you hurt people? Is that your job?

Ian becomes frustrated. He pulls over and drops his head down.

Ian: No! That's not my job! That's nothing you girls need to know!

Alisha: Fine! We were just asking. It would be nice to know what you do and not be treated like kids. Stop lying to us when we can clearly see what's going on!

Erin:(softly says) Please don't lie to us, Big I. Have character.

Ian: (smirking) Have character.

They sit in silence for a minute.

Ian: (calmly) Okay. You are right. I'm sorry for yelling at you and Erin.

Erin: It's okay.

Ian: This could get dangerous quick, and it's only fair to tell you guys the severity of this. In order to keep you safe, I need to be able to tell you what I expect from you both if we ever get into a crisis. Is that fair?

Alisha: Yes! So, you'll answer some of our questions?

Ian: No. You won't be asking questions, but I will tell you a short story of what I do and how I started doing all this. I'll share why your mom and Brian asked me to drive you instead of taking you themselves. We'll stop and get some lunch up the road here. I'll have to get some gas here soon too. Okay?

Erin: Okay, I can't wait to hear the story. I love story time!

Alisha: Thank you, Daddy. You can actually go to this pizza diner in Iowa; they have a gas station connected too.

Ian: How do you know that? You have never been to Iowa or to Minnesota. At least your mom never mentioned you went.

Erin: We have never been to Minnesota.

Alisha: Oh, uh, I have a friend who once told me about it going up this way.

Ian: (confused) Alisha. You didn't know what highway 70 was just three hours ago.

Alisha: Yes, I did. I was just joking, daddy. (Forcefully laughing)

Ian: Um, hmm. Ok.

Ian starts the car, and they head back on the road. They arrive at a pizza shop and gas station. Alisha hurried up and texted Nicole their location and where they were heading.

Erin: I love pizza.

Ian: I love pizza too. What topping is your favorite?

Erin: My favorite topping is cheese.

Ian: Just cheese?

Erin: Yes! I love cheese.

Ian: Ok, and Alisha, I'm sure you want pepperoni, right?

Alisha: Yes, Daddy, I would like pepperoni.

Ian gets out and begins to pump gas. Ian then goes to the trunk and opens his suitcase. In the suitcase, he grabs a scanning device that gives him a 3-D layout of the diner. He then tracks where the exits are and where the restroom is. He also doesn't see any hidden compartments or rooms. As Ian walks back to the gas pump, the girls sit in the car.

Erin: Have you been here before?

Alisha: No, but I do remember seeing this. Whatever happens, stay away from that red truck parked over to our right.

Erin: Why?

Alisha: We just need to stay away from it, Erin.

Erin: Okay. Did you tell Mom?

Alisha: Shhh. Don't say that too loud. I'm not supposed to have the phone, but I'm about to text her to let her know we made it.

Ian:(Finished using the gas pump, opens up Alisha's side of the door.) Okay, let's get some pizza real quick and head back on the road. Also, don't talk to anyone in here but me, okay? We don't know who's watching us. And use our very low, inside voices when we eat at the table. Use the restroom when we go inside. I'll wait for you, then we will order. Okay?

Erin: What if I don't have to go to the pot?

Ian: Try Erin, we've been in the car for a while, and I know you have to at least try, okay?

Alisha: I'll take her too, Dad. I have to go as well.

Ian: Thank you, Alisha. (smiling) I'll stand by for you girls at the entrance and scope everything out.

They walk into the pizza diner. All eyes in the diner turn to them. Alisha and Erin locate the restroom in the back right corner and walk towards it. Ian then watches some other customers. They have a bar and an arcade. He's scoping out the environment. He observes for any unusual character. He sees a sheriff sitting at the bar. He sees a television in the dining area. They have a sports channel on TV. He doesn't get any unnatural feeling and is at ease. He looks outside the window and notices that the clouds are moving south, but he does not worry. Finally, the girls return to him from the restroom.

Ian: You girls good?

Erin: Yes. You don't have to use the pot, Big I?

Ian: No, I'm fine, little E, thank you

They approach the hostess behind the bar.

Ian: (Greets the hostess) Good afternoon, ma'am. You guys really upgraded in here. It has been a while since I've been here. Didn't have the arcade and bar here last time. It's nice.

Hostess: Good afternoon, sir. Welcome to the pizza diner. Thanks, by the way. And yeah, it gets very busy around the lunch hour. And look at these two pretty girls here. What're your names, little girls?

Ian: This is El, and the taller one is Alice.

Erin: My name is Erin.

Ian: (Eyes wide) Ha, ha. She wants to be an Erin so much.

Hostess: Ha. That's okay, El. I would like to be Sheila, but everyone insists on calling me Lela. (laughing)

Ian: (forced laughter) Aw, that's a good one. Could we get a table, please, and get a large cheese pizza and a large pepperoni pizza?

Erin: And that powder cheese, too, please.

Lela: You mean Parmesan, sweetheart. That's fine. You all can sit at table 10. And I'll put that order in for you now.

Ian: Thank you.

They walk to table ten and sit down.

Ian: Erin, remember what I said. Only talk to me.

Erin: Sorry. I forgot.

Ian: That's okay, just remember next time.

Erin: Yes, sir. (looking sad)

Ian: Erin, Alisha tells me you don't think I like you.

Erin: (eyes wide) Alisha, you told him! (bashful)

Ian: It's okay. I'm not upset, and I don't hate you, Erin. I think you are a funny, smart kid.

(Erin and Alisha smile.)

Erin: You do?

Ian: Yes, I think it's brave, and nice that you want to go on this trip with us. I just want you to know that if you ever see me upset or angry, it's not because of you; it's just grown-up things cause issues. Usually, kids like yourselves are always caught in the middle of the grown-up mess. Do you understand?

Erin: I think so.

Ian: When you get older, you'll see what I mean. But anyway, no, Erin, I do not hate you, your mom, or your dad. I just have things that I sometimes can't let go of. We had a great conversation last night, though, that, I believe, was a start to better our relationship.

Erin: Why are you and mommy not married? And why did Alisha and I have two different Dads? Why did my dad be my Dad, and why are you Alisha's dad?

Ian: Okay, wow. I wasn't expecting you to ask that. Um, okay. I think this is a better question when your Mom, your Dad, and I are all together to tell the story. Just so you can hear from all sides.

Alisha: Mom already told us it was a huge mistake on all ends. But you all moved past it.

Ian: A huge mistake on all ends? Let me start by saying your mother is a good woman. That was the reason I fell in love with her. She was funny, smart, caring, understanding, and beautiful. She also had a strong will. She was so sure with who she was and what she wanted, especially in a man. So, when I turned into a "recruiter" she was very supportive. When we first got married, I was gone a lot. I did a lot of training for this job, then had a few assignments around the world. I was helping people, managing people, reuniting families. I did my job at a high level. But as I was saving the world, my world became in danger.

Erin: In danger? (curious)

Ian: In other words, Erin, it became hard to manage and keep your mother happy, me as well. And Alisha, around this time, you were asking about me a lot, needing me a lot. I missed your first steps, your first full sentence, and even missed a few birthdays.

Alisha: (With her head down) That's okay, Daddy. You're a very busy man.

Ian: The crazy part about that, Alisha, is that I still miss things. But we've talked about that earlier, my love.

Alisha: Yes, we have. (smiling)

Ian: So anyway, Erin. With your Mom and Alisha, home alone all the time. Your Mom met your Dad. She met Brian, and he was able to do for her that I wasn't able to.

Erin: And what's that?

Ian: Just be there. Make time for her and your sister. So, this is where you came along.

Alisha: While you and Mom were together? Are you serious? Daddy, I never knew that. (Visibly disturbed)

Erin: What does that mean? Alisha, why are you getting upset?

Alisha: Because Mom cheat-

Ian: Alisha, it's okay. No need to get worked up.

Alisha: No! Dad, mom, has been lying this whole time to us, saying that you two just got a divorce, and I never understood why? Mom has been lying.

Erin: Is mommy a hypofit?

Ian: Umm. No, Erin, she's not a hypocrite. And, Alisha, you need to watch your words when it pertains to your Mother! (Ian softly says)

Alisha: (folding her arms) Fine. Okay.

Ian: Listen, the both of you need to understand that what your mother did was a mistake. We all make mistakes. I've made plenty myself. But apologizing and being sincere with it is what we have done. From all parties. Brian, your Mom and me. All is forgiven, and we are moving forward, especially for the sake of you two. So don't disrespect your Mom, Alisha. Do we have an understanding?

Alisha: Yeah.

Ian: Excuse me?

Alisha: Yes, sir, I'm sorry.

Ian: Thank you. That is what happened between us, though, Erin. But your mom and Dad have made a beautiful family and are doing a great job raising you two. Love them and always be thankful for them. They do all they can to show you two as much love as possible. Any more questions, Erin or Alisha?

Erin: Yes. How did I get here?

Ian: We just drove here, Erin. What do you mean? (Chuckling)

Erin: No, like how was I born?

Ian: Oh! Well, that's definitely a question you should only ask your Mom or Dad. Trust me on that, Little E.

Alisha laughs.

Erin: Okay. When can you tell us another story?

Alisha: Yeah, Dad, tell us exactly how you got the job you do now. Because I've been telling my friends that you are a delivery driver and sort of a job recruiter.

Ian: Well, I was a driver. My position title says recruiter now, technically. But it's more to my job description than what I said earlier. I save people, help people, and beat up the bad guys. Try to make the world a better place day by day. I tell you what; I'll tell you the story of when I started my job, then we have to get back on the road. Cool?

Alisha and Erin both nod their heads yes.

Ian: Okay, cool. Erin, are you listening? Let me know if you get bored; it will be a short but detailed story, okay?

Erin: Okay.

Alisha: Well, get ready to go back to sleep, Erin.

Ian: Hush. Story time!

CHAPTER 5

Shadow Child

Ian: So, as you both know, I work for a delivery company called Zip, right?

Alisha and Erin nod.

Ian: Okay. Well, before I started there, I had to do a little growing. Go through school, and things, just like you girls do now.

Erin: Did you have a mom and dad like us?

Ian: Well, yes, everybody has a mom or dad. I was about nine, when my biological parents were killed. I didn't know until a few years later. I had thought they just abandoned me and didn't love me anymore. I was going on a field trip that day, and I remember my parents kissing me goodbye that morning and dropping me off at school, but never came back to pick me up from school.

Alisha: Why did you think they had left you?

Ian: I don't know why I thought that. They never gave me a reason to feel unloved. They always showed me love and all up to their disappearance. I can just remember sitting and waiting for one of them to show up. But neither ever came. I still remember my mom's scent and my Dad shining his shoes that morning.

Alisha: What were their names?

Ian: Joseph and Sarah. Names I could never forget.

Alisha: Sorry, Dad. I never knew this.

Ian: It's okay. But from then on, I was in a foster home. I will admit, for a while, I thought my mom and dad would come back. My first foster home, a family, took me in named the Lowes. An older couple with no children. The Lowes were strict but disciplined. Taught me many things. Helped me deal with a lot of my anger. Hard, tough love, but love nonetheless. Even when I tried pushing them away emotionally, they were helping me make progress. "Moving forward was the key," that's what Mr. Lowe would say. I would ignore the advice they would give, but they never gave up on me. Then the dreams began, those dreams that you both are beginning to have now. These dreams showing my powers or giving me a glimpse of what was to come. They didn't understand, just like I didn't, but they were helping me try to understand what was going on with me. They were trying to convince me, I could use these powers for some type of good.

Erin: What were your foster parents' names?

Ian: My foster father was Warrick Lowe, and my foster mother was Everett Lowe. They defended me until they died.

Alisha: How did they pass? (Worried look)

Ian: The Dream Man. He was tracking me, watching me in my dreams. You know, Alisha, how I talk about the dreams that lead me to discover my power. How would I be on this pathway leaving Earth? I was running away from something, but I didn't realize it until I saw him for the first time. He would get closer and closer each time I would dream. It was a nightmare when everything would be bright, colorful and then turn shadowy. Once I saw the shadow, I knew it was him. Never seen his face, never wanted to. So, I would run and run, and run until I realized I was running up towards the sky where I met a bright star. The Star led me to the Sun.

Alisha: The Sun? Like the physical Sun?

Erin: Was it hot?

Ian: Yes, the actual Sun. And yes, it was definitely hot. I am uncertain what the sun really looks like this close-up, but it had a beautiful glow. Fiery, of course, but it was so beautiful. It looked like a big star itself. And it was so shiny and intense. Well, as I faced the sunlight, the shadowy figure or the Dream Man had made its way to the Sun too. But I think the Sun felt that darkness heading its way. Mind you, it's already like pitch black in outer space, but that's how bright the sun can get. It got so bright that it brought that dark shadow out to the light. Brighten up so much, and it turned the shadow away.

Erin: The Sun did that?

Ian: Yes, the sun did. This is all in my dream, too, of course. But it felt so real. The Sun then put the Star that led me to it, placed the Star over my heart. Now that part burn and is painful. But it felt so rewarding, too. I felt like I had accomplished something in my life. It felt like things were looking up, and I was going to beat the shadow that stayed with me and finally break through. It's hard getting the shadows off you.

Alisha: So you did, right?

Ian: No, not exactly. That next day was when my foster parents died. They never woke up. The police and the autopsy couldn't explain the sudden death. But I knew how; I knew the truth. Dream Man got to them, trying to get to me. I don't know what happened in their dreams, or maybe they had something he actually wanted. He is someone I never thought I would run into again. I still don't intend to run into him now.

Erin: Can we please stop talking about him? He really scares me.

Ian: I know little E. He terrified me too. I was scared to sleep for a very long time. But eventually, I figured out a way to keep him from my dreams. That was not going to sleep. So, I began sleeping for an hour every day. Then I managed to make it an hour every 7. So, 3 hours I would get rest.

Alisha: I need my sleep. How did that even work with school and things?

Ian: It didn't. I started to slack in school because of it. I think most teachers felt sorry for me and my situation, so they just passed me by to the next grade. I wanted to give up each day, thinking that he would find me. I remained in fear, and I was paranoid. That was my life from twelve years old until I was seventeen. Lived in different foster cares in the city. No one could get through to me, not like the Lowes. And honestly, I didn't want them to, either. I wanted to just drown in my sorrows and stay afraid. I also stopped believing my biological parents would come back for me, too.

Alisha: But you had your powers then too. You could have protected yourself after all that.

Ian: I didn't care for my powers then. Especially not how I do now. Kind of how you feel about them.

Alisha: Yeah, good riddance to them.

Ian: Anyway, I still didn't understand how the powers worked or how to use them. I went back to being angry again, too, more of a "why does this keep happening to me? What did I do to deserve this pain." That is what I would ask myself, going to get my hour's rest. I also had to stay calm because the parents I stayed with then weren't as nice and less tolerant. I can remember getting so angry trying to explain why my grades were bad to my new family that I stormed out of the house. My Foster dad, Marcus, tried to stop me from leaving that he felt how hot I had gotten when he grabbed me by the shoulder. The look on his face when he saw my eyes. I couldn't see anything but red, too. So to keep myself cool and never show my powers, I just hid them. It was very hot out that day, and the sun was not letting up. But it was like the Sun wanted me to unleash something inside me, to finally let out all that emotion I was bottling up. I was able to get my head cleared, but it was too late. That family didn't want to deal with me anymore after that. So I moved with another family after that. By this point, I knew I had deep scars. I was angry, had silent hatred in my heart, and silently crying for guidance.

Alisha: Why didn't you just ask for help? Or tell anyone?

Ian: I didn't know how to ask for it. I almost wanted to give up on everything, too. I didn't see any happiness or hope until my senior year at school when I met your mother.

Erin: You and Mom met in school?

Ian: Yes, we did. We met during lunch. I would see her all throughout our high school years, but never said anything to her. Honestly, I said nothing to anyone. But you know your mother, she's friendly and can talk or make conversation with anyone.

Alisha: That's definitely, mom.

Ian: Right. So, she came and asked to sit at the table with me. She vowed to make new friends in her senior year and get to know everyone in our class. So, she asked me about myself.

I was first reluctant and dismissive. I didn't want people to know anymore about me. Or being afraid of me, too. Nicole told me a little bit about herself. Her family, what she wanted to do, what college she was going to. She just talked and talked. By the end of lunch. She said she would be back tomorrow to do it again.

Alisha: Did she?

Ian: I tried to sit at another table, but she found me. Sat down, talked some more and asked more questions. (laughing) I still wasn't answering them. Well, I would give her one-word answers. I thought she was just nosey and very annoying. So that Wednesday and Thursday, I sat at my locker and ate lunch. I figured she would try to find me, but she didn't. So then I felt she would forget about me or take a hint. But guess what?

Alisha: What happened?

Erin: What?

Ian: She spotted me on that Friday. (laughing) She says, "I found you. You probably think I'm a stalker." I mean, I did just a slight bit, but she finally got me to crack a smile. So we talked a little bit. I told her what classes I had and other things. Well, at the end of lunch, she asked if I had any plans that evening? I told her I did have to work. Your mother says, "Well, we have a church event this evening; you are more than welcome to join. Games, food, and fellowship." I didn't know what to say. I was kind of taken back.

Alisha: Why?

Erin: What is fellowship?

Ian: I was taken back by how kind your mother was. Sometimes the world isn't a nice, kind place, so for your mother to be a vessel of extending love and gratitude meant a lot. And Erin, fellowship means being friendly with one another and towards the group that you are around. So, you would have fellowship with your friends when you play with dolls. Do you understand?

Erin: I think so.

Ian: That's okay; you girls will get it someday. But anyway, I told your mother I would love to come and thanked her for the kind gesture. Unfortunately, I was in need of money. I was turning eighteen, which means I was aging out of foster care. My foster parents at that time told me I could stay much longer if I needed to after I aged out, but I just felt it was best to be on my own. Nicole understood and actually felt bad. She felt like she had met a friend, and I felt as if I was gaining my first friend in a long time.

She asked where I worked, and I told her I worked for the Arch west post dispatch.

Alisha: Who is that?

Ian: That was our paper company before these phones took over the news media. I had been working there during the nights for a year around that time. My foster dad, John, got me on. He knew I was sleep-deprived and recommended working a job that would tire me out. He also thought it would be therapeutic since I wouldn't seek guidance for my sleep deprivation. And honestly, the paper company was tiring, and it was also therapeutic too. It took me away from my troubles and thoughts. Gave me some type of purpose, it felt like.

Alisha: Did you ride a bike? (laughing)

Ian:(laughing) I actually did. I would help prong the paper the journalist would write that day or that night. Then I would ride my bike around throwing paper from 1 to 5 in the morning. I would get back home, sleep for an hour, shower, and get ready for school.

Alisha: What about weekends?

Ian: I would work. Sometimes workout, try to stay fit. Practice my karate or routine I learned years before with my Lowe family. Most of the time would be bored. And also ride my bike. The thing I wanted to do most, though I would sleep, I couldn't and knew I couldn't. I don't know how I survived at that time. Well, I take that back; I do know.

Alisha: How?

Ian: Not to sound corny, but once again, your mother. She and her family. After the church event that I wasn't able to attend, they came and helped me deliver the papers. This was where I truly understood what a family and a bond were. Meeting your grandparents and seeing how they interacted with your mother.

Erin: Grandpa and Grandma!

Ian: Yes, ma'am. They are still some of my favorite people to this day. When I first met Mr. Robert and Mrs. Ella. They showed love to me instantly. They helped that night and almost took away all of my thoughts, anger, and sadness for a little time. I got done so early that they took me to a twenty-four-hour breakfast spot. I had pancakes, and I felt safe and wanted for the first time in a long time. I also felt loved. Just from that first interaction with them. They prayed for me and invited me to church. Mr. Rob told me no pressure, of course, but all I wanted to do was be around them after that Friday night. And that I was. Began visiting them on a regular for Bible study and got to know Nicole a lot better too. Nicole had reached her goal; she gained a new friend. I finally found a friend that I didn't want to be separated from. Her parents noticed that too, and they noticed how happy we were together when we spent time together. She really made me forget about that pain before her. She tutored me to help get my grades up. I didn't share everything with them, but I shared my secret gift with Nicole. She was supportive and very encouraging, looking at it as a gift. She prayed with me on facing my fears, embracing my truth, and protecting the Legacy and plans God had for me. I never grew up religious or believing in a higher power. But she and your grandparents helped me on trusting and believing in him. They didn't force it on me; they just prayed that I someday would.

Alisha: Now that you say that, Dad, I've never heard you talk about God or see you go to church.

Ian: I know. You probably never will, too. I've done things for which I now feel there's no redemption or forgiveness.

Erin: God always forgives Big I.

Ian: (Smiling) Thank you for that, Erin. And I sure hope so. Maybe someday I'll get back to that. It's just hard, too. Anyway, things started getting more serious with Nicole and I, but I think we were both unfamiliar with that, and we procrastinated with that. So, Mr. Rob took me to lunch one day on a Saturday. He told me I was like the son he never had. I was kind and respectful to Mrs. Ella. And I became Nicole's best friend; he knows Nicole truly has feelings for me and sees I do too for her. So, Mr. Rob says. "Ian, time waits for no one. People move on, just like times and just like blessings. God has blessed Nicole with providing a friend like you. But my daughter will be a great woman, and the best wife God could bless a man with. Not saying you all should get married tomorrow, but to see if you both might like each other more is worth a try. And don't worry, Ella is having the same talk with Nicole. Just think about it, Ian."

Alisha: Mommy has never told us this; this sounds like a whole different person from what we see.

Ian: How so?

Alisha: Mom sounds happy. It just sound like she used to have fun too.

Ian: Really? I'm sure your mom is tired a lot.

Alisha: I guess. Just seems like, maybe we took the fun away from her.

Ian: No, that's not the case. You two are all she talks about. Like I mentioned before, things sometimes just happen. Let me ask you girls this. Do you still go to church?

Alisha: Yes, sir.

Erin: Yes.

Ian: Okay. Do you girls still pray when you wake up, before you eat, and before you go to bed?

Alisha: Yeah.

Erin: (Eating pizza) Yes.

Ian: Then your mom sounds like the same woman I fell in love with because I still do those things. Remember that your mom has made some mistakes, and so have I. But you, Alisha, are eleven going on twelve. And Erin, you're five going on six. You both will make mistakes too, maybe and hopefully not the same as us. But it happens. And you don't want to be judged on your mistakes. Mistakes and failure build character; perfection isn't a character at all. Remember that, girls. And if you don't get it now, you will when you get older. But anyway, so I finally asked your mother on a date. She excitedly said yes. We went on a Saturday afternoon to a pizza restaurant called Mr. Pizza. Then we walked around the mall and got ice cream. Had a good, fun time.

Alisha: (smiling) How did you get there?

Ian: We took the bus; no shame in that. Have you not heard any of our dates and stories?

Alisha: Not at all. You are constantly working, and so does Mom. Grandma and Grandpa always ask how you are; they sometimes say they miss you and pray that you are doing well. I never knew everything was so perfect before.

Ian: Oh, it wasn't perfect, but those are stories for a later time. But your mother and I fell in love, and we went to prom together; I celebrated all the holidays with the family. To be honest with you, I was probably at my happiest at that time. I mean, I'm fine now and all, but what your Nicole and her parents did for me and showed me was nothing I experienced. They showed what a foundation should look like. I will be forever grateful for that, and they pulled me out of a deep hole. Didn't happen overnight, but it did happen.

Alisha: So why do you two argue or get upset with each other so much now?

Ian: Mainly, it's over you and our co-parenting decisions. But your mother and I have been through a lot together. She's seen a lot of good from me and seen me at my worst, and this is after that hole I was pulled from. Your mother knows me better than anyone; my job puts a lot of stress on me, and occasionally I have to go back to that dark place where I grew up to get certain jobs done. Certain things I'm not proud of, and some things I am. It doesn't help, though, when I come back home, I notice that home is no different from out there.

Erin: What's out there?

Ian: Chaos, little one, sometimes home and the world can just be plain old chaos. It's about time to go; I'll share a bit of what I do in the car. That's for your ears only, girls.

CHAPTER 6

※

Clouds Travel

Alisha: Wow, Dad! That was actually a lovely story. Can't wait to hear what you do for work. That is what you truly do. We didn't fall asleep from boredom, too. (Laughing)

Ian: Ha Ha Ha. Thank you, that's only part of it. You will learn more later. Let's go, okay.

Erin: I have to use the pot.

Alisha: I'll take her Dad. I have to go too.

Ian: Okay. Don't take too long. We sat a little longer than we needed to. I'm going to pay and be waiting for you at the front counter.

Alisha and Erin walk to the restroom, and Ian walks to the cash register. The sheriff, still sitting at the bar, turns to Ian and the girl's direction. He's observing them and smiles. Ian notices the sheriff is watching them.

Ian: Excuse me, miss Lela.

Lela: Yes, sir?

Ian: How much for the pizzas?

Lela: Oh, well, let me get your check. One minute, sir, I'll be right back.

Ian: You know what, ma'am, the pizzas were so good, and the girls enjoyed it so much… (pulls out a $100 bill) Keep the change. Your service was excellent.

Lela: Oh my goodness, thank you so much, sir. May God bless you and your girls. This means a lot.

Sheriff: (watching, speaks with a southern accent) Mighty generous. You girls got a good father raising you.

Erin: Actually, he's not my Dad.

Ian: Erin, shh.

Sheriff: Oh really? It must be your uncle.

Ian: (Ignoring sheriff) Thank you, ma'am. Have a lovely day.

Sheriff: Storm passing through in about ten minutes coming from the north.

Ian: Probably best to get to going then. Thanks for the heads-up, sir. (Begins walking away with Alisha and Erin.)

Sheriff: No problem, Ian!

(Alisha and Erin stop walking. Ian continues to ignore him and keeps walking.)

Ian: (Under his breath) Keep walking and hang close by.

Alisha: (Scared look) Dad. He knows your name.

Ian: Stand close by; he doesn't know me.

Sheriff: Sure, don't, but I know that's Alisha and Erin. Those girls of yours. We have been looking for them.

Ian: They're fine, "Sheriff." Alisha, Erin, let's go now!

Erin begins to walk toward Ian

Ian: Alisha. Come on, please. We need to go!

Sheriff: (Scoffs) I'm no sheriff. Why would you think that? Oh, maybe the hat and outfit give that away. No, no, no. Not at all. Just a southern feller, last of my kind, actually. Names Walton.

Ian: Okay, Walton. I already figured you weren't one. I'm pretty sure who you are here for and on whose behalf. We don't need to go down this road. Now Alisha. Let's go for the last time!

Walton: Ian. She's scared, trembling. Little miss, Alisha. I don't want you. I'm actually-

Ian: (getting frustrated) I'm going to stop you there. We're leaving Walton, or we can pick up this outside if need be. No one in here needs to get hurt, especially innocent people.

Lela: Yeah, take this outside, guys. Trying to run a business. Since I know, you're not a cop. I'll call the cops too.

Walton: You stay out of this, ma'am! Besides, the law ain't showing up anytime soon. Let's just say they are a long way from here.

Lela and the other customers were confused.

Ian: So you probably hurt, or worse, killed the town's officers.

Walton: Bingo! Seem like a smart man, Ian. I require the girl. I don't intend to harm anyone else. I'm just doing my job. Doing what's asked of me by my boss.

Ian: From the Dream Man.

Walton: Funny. I gave him the same name too.

Ian: He can't do it himself and needs a lackey to do his dirty work in the real world. Doesn't get his hands dirty here. That's fine; I have a a responsibility to do as well. And that's protecting these girls at all costs.

Walton: Ok, last chance. We can even negotiate.

Ian: What? Negotiate? I tell you what, come near these girls, and those will be your last steps, man.

Walton: Your threats don't bother me. But yeah, negotiate. See, I know you're heading up to Minnesota. See, your ex-wife spilled the beans. We have her and her husband, Brian. Paid them a visit about an hour after you all left this morning. They never got the chance to make it to her parents. Some of my men came by last night and were killed. You did a good job trying to hide them, but we found them anyway. Give me the girls, and I'll make sure that Nicole and Brian will be spared.

Ian: And how did you know where to find us in this pizza diner? They had no clue where we would be. So, I call a bluff.

Walton: Tracker! That's easy. Little miss Alisha, there's been texting and keeping her mom updated.

Alisha: Sorry, Daddy. (Beginning to cry)

Ian: It'll be okay, baby. We're getting out of this.

Walton: You sure? I mentioned those clouds are coming this way, which means your little powers won't work. Can't do much without the sun, can you? But my powers have no limitations or requirements. I'm all ready to go. So, are you certain you want to go down that road?

Ian: And what can you do, Old Gunslinger?

Walton stretches his body from the waist up; he then lunges his top half towards Ian and hits Ian with his shoulders. This knocks the girl's backwards and knocks Ian outside the diner window. Alisha falls back and hits a table. While Erin fell on some bystanders in the diner. Walton then walks out the diner's front door and straightens his collar.

Walton: Old isn't the word I would use. How 'bout "Aged Gunslinger?" Straight from the South! Yee haw. Are negotiations closed?

(Ian notices he isn't too injured, looks up to the sky and sees some sunlight.)

Ian: Not just yet!

Walton: (laughs) Oh, you really are something; you should have at least a broken rib. Nothing? (glancing up to the sky) Aw, so you have some sun left out about. The clouds are passing through now. God, don't let it rain; you will really be at a real disadvantage. Might want to figure something out quick then.

Ian: (Picking himself up from the ground) I've been figuring things out since you first looked at us. I'm well-prepared.

Walton: We'll see!

Walton charges toward Ian with a right hook; Ian dodges the hook and connects with a left body uppercut, lifting Walton from his feet with the uppercut; Ian then lifts his right knee with force to the gut of Walton. Still lifted off his feet, Walton is sent flying a few feet away from Ian; after Ian delivers a spinning back elbow.

Ian runs back towards the diner to check on Alisha and Erin.

Ian: Girls! Alisha! Erin! Where are you?

Lela: They're over here.

Alisha and Erin holding one another, crying.

Ian: Damn. Are you both okay? Come on, girls, we need to get out of here now. It's going to be okay.

Ian notices Alisha has a bruise on her face. Ian becomes even angrier, at seeing the bruise.

Ian: Look at my baby's face.

Lela: I've tried calling 911. No one's answering.

Ian: He's taken out this town communication, dispatch included. He wasn't lying; you guys are here alone. Someone needs to post this online.

Walton lunges back into the diner.

Walton: No need, no one's coming. And that little combo of yours hurt. Not happening agai-

Ian charges toward Walton with a flying kick, which kicks him back outside. Ian sees he has little sunlight left near a red truck. He has to think of his next move quickly before Walton gets back up. Ian wants to stay on the offense but can't, so he has to get defensive.

Alisha, Erin, and a few other strangers run outside. Alisha and Erin rush towards Ian's truck. Some customers run towards their cars to get away. But out of nowhere, Walton stretches his left arm out to about fifty feet; he jumbles the cars of the customers trying to flee together, then slides them towards the girls. Ian runs fast as he can, and dives for them, saving them from the cars. The cars and the customers get swung into the pizza diner. Ian and the girls run towards the red truck and hid behind the passenger side.

Walton: Don't hide now; where's that tough talk at? Oh, that's right, those clouds have gotten in the way now.

Ian tries to find some sunlight left out in the field. Erin and Alisha both are crying and whimpering.

Walton: Sounds like you got some scared girls there. It's ok, girls. I will get you to safety. Hahaha! This is all your parent's fault. People are getting hurt and dying.

Alisha: Just leave us alone, please!

Walton: I got a job to do, sweetheart. This is partially your fault too. But I thank you, it will be all over soon. Are you done fighting now, Ian? Let's get this over with so I can be on my way.

Ian: (telling Alisha and Erin) When I run out towards that little bit of sunlight, you two run towards my truck.

Alisha: Daddy, please don't leave us. We can't run to your truck; we are not that fast.

Ian: You don't need to; you just need to follow my instructions and listen to everything I tell you to do. When you get to the truck, open the trunk and open my suitcase. The code will be the day before your birthday to open it up. Understand?

Alisha: Uh-

Ian: Alisha, it's ok to be afraid, but that man is trying to kill us; I need you to focus and get your sister across there. Do you understand? Don't stop until you get there.

Erin: (whimpering) We can do this, Alisha. I will run fast too.

Ian: You both got this.

Walton: Damn, you are stubborn (looks at Lela, who's in the truck, fiddling for her keys in her purse.) And you got another civilian to protect.

Ian: Okay! Walton! We're coming out. Don't hurt my girls or the waitress. One on one, and let's finish this.

Walton: (smiling) Now, you're talking. Get on out here and let's get this over with.

As Ian steps out and charges toward Walton, Alisha, and Erin run towards the truck. Walton extends his right arm toward the girls, and his left fist is extending toward Ian. Ian dodges the punch but catches Walton's arm.

Ian: Girls, slide now!

As Alisha and Erin slide, they both dodge Walton's right arm, trying to catch them. The girls continue to run. Ian is snatched back with Walton's left arm. As he is coming back, he hits Walton with a right jab. Ian goes for another jab, but his fist is grabbed by Walton's left hand. Walton then knees Ian in his left rib, followed by a punch that sends Ian flying back. But Ian is caught by Walton's right arm, and Ian is sent speeding back towards the bottom of Walton's left boot.

Walton: I told you, boy, this would not end well for you.

Ian then rolls into some sunlight as Walton is about to stomp on him. Walton runs toward Ian, but is caught off guard by a spinning back elbow from Ian.

Ian: Didn't see that coming, huh?

Walton: (spits out tooth) I didn't. Some move there (as he looks at Ian's feet, he notices some sunlight). Aww, that's how, huh?

Ian: Just wait for those clouds to clear. Might not be able to kill you yet! But this will do for now.

Walton: Not unless I knock you out of that circle of sunlight.

Ian: Let's see.

Meanwhile, Alisha and Erin make it to Ian's truck. Erin gets in the back seat. While Alisha goes to the trunk and finds Ian's suitcase. She uses the code to unlock it.

Alisha: 04012011. It's not working. Daddy! It's not working!

Ian dodges Walton's punches, trying to stay in the sunlight circle.

Ian: Month, date, year!

Alisha: Huh?

Ian: MONTH! DATE! YEAR!

Alisha: I did. It's not working.

Ian: Did you put 2011 instead of just 11?

Alisha: Ugh. Yeah! Sorry!

Ian: That's o. That's okay, just hurry on up.

Walton: Yeah, hurry. Daddy doesn't have much time left. Hahaha.

Lela finally finds her keys and starts her car. Then BOOM! Walton punches through Lela's truck, damaging it. Lela gets out and begins to run towards Ian's truck.

Walton: You are making me work today; been a while since I've had a fight like this.

Walton tries to land another punch with his right, but Ian catches it. While Ian has that right, Walton comes with a left hook, but that is caught as well. As Walton brings his arms back towards himself, Ian doesn't let go of Walton's arms, coming back with them. Ian then kicks both feet up together and connects with a drop-kick to Walton's face, breaking his nose and stunning him.

Walton: (holding on to his nose) My nose! I think you broke my nose!

Ian then begins running towards his truck, but also notices Lela running next to him. As Ian continues to run, Walton throws rocks and punches, stretching his legs, and kicking dirt up towards Ian to stop him from getting to his truck. But Ian dodges everything and gets to his truck. Lela gets some dirt kicked up towards her eyes.

Walton: What's in your trunk must be something mighty important.

Ian tries to navigate Lela towards his truck.

Ian: Keep running straight, Lela. You are almost here.

Lela begins to drift left towards the diner.

Ian: No, Lela! Run slightly more to your right! Lela, follow my voice.

Lela continues to drift more left.

Lela: Where are you? I don't know whe-

Ian: Watch out!

Lela runs into the diner's brick wall.

Ian: Damn. (Then turns to get to his trunk)

Alisha: Daddy, watch ou-

Walton appears behind the truck with Ian. He then takes a few swings at Ian. Ian is able to dodge the punches. Ian grabs his suitcase and hits Walton with it. Alisha opens the driver's side and get in the truck. Erin continues to scream in fear.

Ian: Are you girls in?

Alisha: Yes.

Ian: Good, lock the doors.

Alisha: But what about you?

Ian: I'll be fine, Just-

Walton backhands the suitcase away from Ian. The suitcase land by Lela's red truck. Walton then grabs and picks Ian up and punches him back towards the diner.

Alisha: Dad!

Erin: (Screaming) Big I!

Walton: Shut it!

Walton goes for the door, but Alisha starts the truck and puts the truck in gear and begins to drive. Walton catches the back bumper and holds

on. Ian gets back up slowly to see Alisha trying to drive off. Ian looks beside him; Lela is dead, but she has her keys in her hands. Ian grabs her keys and runs towards her truck.

Walton: Where you going, Ian? Just going to leave the girls (laughing)

Alisha: Daddy!

Ian reaches for his suitcase, grabs a small can out of it, and throws it in the air. He then grabs his gun and shoots at the can, which explodes. This distracts Walton, and he lets go of the truck.

Walton: (visibly upset and annoyed) Dammit! Just stop! Get back here!

As Ian is about to get in Lela's truck with the suitcase, Walton stretches his arms out and catches Ian right before he reaches the truck. As Alisha is driving, swerving to get to the truck, she sees Walton's arms flying back towards them with Ian. Alisha instantly pushes on the brakes.

Alisha: Ok, Erin, now we can go to the red truck. Get in and don't come out until Dad and I get back.

Erin: Alisha, please don't leave me! What if you don't come back?

Alisha: We will be back. I've seen it just like this. Okay, E. We'll be okay. I just have to time it just right and find something to hold the gear down. (Alisha looks in her bag and grabs the brick.) This will do.

Ian reaches back to Walton. Walton wraps Ian around him in a bear hug and squeezes Ian's back towards him while the suitcase is on Ian's chest. Ian has his gun tightly wrapped in his right hand.

Walton: This is how it ends. Must admit, you were a formative foe. Been a long time.

Ian: (losing oxygen, gasping for air) Ahh. (He remembers he has something in the suitcase that might slow Walton down.)

Walton: Just breathe. It will be all over in just a few seconds.

Ian: Not just yet.

Ian leans his head back and tries to go for a headbutt. Walton knows this and stretches his neck back. This gives Ian a little wiggle room to drop the suitcase and shoot the gun near Walton's left foot. Walton drops Ian. Walton's neck comes back towards his body. Ian opens the suitcase quickly.

Walton: You missed

Ian: I know

Ian grabs a metal ball that is heavy when not in its case. Walton punches Ian to the ground, then tries to go for Ian's throat to strangle him. Ian counters it into a flipping arm bar and drops the metal ball on Walton's right Hand. Walton thinks nothing of it and tries to move it, but can't lift his arm up. He also can't pick the metal ball up with his left hand, either.

Walton: What did you do to me? Why can't I move my arm?

Ian: That's a Baoding ball from one of the heaviest metals in the world. You'll be grounded for a while. Honestly, I don't see you moving without having to cut your elastic arm off your body. I didn't want to kill you in front of my girls, but next time I won't be so generous. Let this be a warning. Tell your boss to leave us alone, too.

Walton: How can you lift it, and I can't?

Ian points down at the ground and shows Walton they are standing in a bit of sunshine.

Ian: Those clouds certainly do travel, huh?

Walton desperately reaches out for Ian's neck. Pushing Ian out of the sunlight. Chocking him.

Walton: Spoke too soon, eh? Get this ball off of me now.

Alisha starts Ian's truck up and begins driving it towards Walton. As she gets about thirty feet from them, she sets the brick on the accelerator and jumps out of the truck. The truck hits Walton and sends him stretching away from his arms. He lets go of Ian, but the baoding ball is still lying on Walton's arm.

Alisha: Ouch! That looks like it's hurting him.

Ian: (coughing, gasping for air) Thank you, Sunshine. How did you get the truck to stay in gear?

Alisha: I used that brick in my bag. Told you it would come in handy.

Ian: Yeah, well, I wore him down. Where's your sister? Erin?

Erin jumps out of Lela's truck and runs towards them.

Alisha: Here she comes.

Ian: Let's get out of here before he shows back up. I don't know how long he can stretch.

Alisha: What will happen if he comes back?

Ian: Fire! We burn him with fire, my love. No coming back from that.

Alisha: Um, well, the other thing is we have no car now.

Ian pulls out Lela's truck keys.

As Ian and Alisha get to the truck. Alisha and Erin get teary-eyed.

Ian: You girls, okay?

Alisha: Yes…

Erin: Yes, sir…

Ian: It's okay to cry. That was a scary situation for us. But we made it through. Let's keep moving forward.

Alisha and Erin begin to cry.

Ian: Let it all out, girls. That was tough.

Ian looks at Alisha's face.

Ian: Your face is bruised. When do you heal? I figured it would have been healed by now.

Alisha: Not sure. I will heal and don't notice sometimes.

Ian: Hmm. Okay. (starts the truck up.)

Alisha: What about all of those people in the diner? Are they…? Are they alive still?

Ian: I'm not sure. I'll call around to give someone a heads-up to check on them. Hopefully, they're okay. We have to keep moving, though.

Erin: What about our bags? My dolls?

Ian: Right now, all we need is this suitcase. Everything else is irrelevant. The most important thing is to keep you girls safe. That's what I'm concerned with. Buckle up, back on the road.

CHAPTER 7

Zip

Ian and the girls begin back on the road. Erin is crying, and Alisha is still trying to process what just happened, trying not to hyperventilate.

Ian: Girls, it's okay. I understand; that was a lot to take in. I want you both to breathe. Take a deep breath. You girls did excellent, by the way, too.

Alisha: (Breathing heavily) We for that, Dad. Still very scary. We almost just died. Like you were almost killed. He had you by your throat. He tried to hit us with his stretchy arms. His whole body could bend, stretch, and move. He should go out for the cheerleading team. I wouldn't mind having these powers.

Ian: You don't. We made it through, and we are on our way to Minnesota. You girls should get some sleep. Erin, it would help to get some rest now.

Alisha: We can't sleep after that! Dad, we almost died. I get you might be used to that, but give us a second to breathe.

Ian: Do I need to pull over? Erin, are you okay now?

Erin: (wiping her tears) Yes, sir. Can I say something now, Big I?

Ian: Anything, Little E. Please let me know what's wrong?

Erin: That was so cool! You were like pow, pow. And he was like, ow, ow! You are like a real-life hero. You did flips and can run so fast. Will we be able to do that someday?

Ian: Okay, Erin, calm down. Take a breath. I don't know how to respond to that. You literally were just crying. You must still be in shock.

Erin: I wasn't shocked. He didn't shock me! I'm fine. I'm going to be a big girl like mommy and daddy said.

Ian: Speaking of Mommy. Alisha. Didn't I say you to leave your phone at home?

Alisha: Uh-

Ian: It's not a hard question. Didn't I tell you to leave your phone at home?

Alisha: Yes, sir.

Ian: Give me the phone.

Alisha hands Ian the phone. He breaks it and then throws it out the car windows.

Alisha: Dad?

Ian: Did mom tell you to bring it? Don't lie either. I don't want to be lied to anymore.

Alisha: Yes, sir, she did.

Ian: Okay. That man caught up with us because he was tracking you, Alisha.

Alisha: (head down) I'm sorry, Dad! I just wanted to let Mom know we were okay. She wanted to make sure, too. That everything would be ok.

Ian: I get that, but someone found us. In a diner. In the middle of nowhere! That could've been bad for us. You might not have much to worry about with that healing power. But Erin and I do. And as a father, I still want to keep you protected, too. For some odd reason, I still feel I'm not being told everything.

(Alisha and Erin look at each other.)

Ian: We have another four hours until we get to Minnesota; we'll have to stop somewhere close by, so we can clean up. You girls should get some more rest. I'll wake you girls up in an hour.

Alisha: Dad, we were just trying to be safe-

Ian: That's enough. I'll have a talk with your mother when I find a phone. Time to get some rest.

Erin: Ian?

Ian: Yes, Erin?

Erin: Are you still going to tell us about your job?

Ian: Not right now.

Erin: Please, it will help me go to sleep faster.

Ian: Okay. It will be fast, though. You girls seriously need some rest.

Erin: Okay.

Ian: Alisha. Are you up for this, or are you going to sleep now?

Alisha: I'm up. I'm listening, father (sarcasm)

Ian: That'll get you popped. Not too old to still get popped with that slick tongue.

Erin snickers

Alisha: Whatever. Can you just tell the story?

Ian: So after your mother and I graduated from high school, she went on to go to college, of course. She attended Arch West College Institution, or AWCI for short. She went for business. And even though mommy helped me get my grades back on track and graduate. Schools, look at your totality of high school work. That's why it's important to be on top of all that when you first begin. Stay getting A's, Alisha.

Alisha: We get it.

Ian: So I stayed working for the newspaper company. But saw in the newspaper that the company Zip was hiring full-time drivers. See, around this time, the recession had happened, and people lost jobs, homes, and money. You'll learn about it in school someday. But Zip was ready to hire full-time drivers again or couriers, so I applied and got the job. So it's required in order to drive and obtain a DOT in stage state of Missouri, you need to be 18. So it worked out perfectly. Zip trained me, and I began driving for them full-time a month after graduation. I loved it, too; I worked long, tiring hours, but it was worth it. Made cool money for my age. The money I haven't seen or was used to. I was able to get my own place. Got this truck you see now.

Alisha: You've had this truck since you were eighteen.

Ian: Yeah, it'll be yours when you're able to drive too.

Alisha: Yeah, okay.

Ian: Anyway, I also was able to take your mother out on more dates. Would see your grandparents more often too. That first year there was pretty cool.

Alisha: Did you have your own area you delivered to?

Ian: Initially, no. I first started as a full-time "Rusher."

Erin: What's that?

Ian: A Rusher was someone who takes a few different routes or smaller areas and delivers them as fast as possible. So then I went from being a "Rusher" to a "Roller." And a "Roller" is someone who covers routes that are left behind or need to be replaced for the day. You may have a different route every day, or possibly the same route for the week. A "Roller" can also do a "Rusher's" job as well. "Rollers almost have no limitations, either; they can go up to as many hours a day. They are the only workers in the company that have no work hour restrictions. I made a lot of money being a "Roller."

Alisha: Okay, so when and why did you stop being a "Roller"?

Ian: I wanted something consistent, and the hours got hectic. Your mom and I weren't married yet, so I wanted to spend more time with her. So I just became "Placer."

Alisha: That name is lame compared to the others.

Ian: Yeah, but you are basically placed on a route, and that's your route until you bid or want another position. Being a placer was cool and all. It wasn't as fun as being a "Roller," but I really wanted to be a Shifter.

Alisha: And what's a shifter?

Ian: That's pretty much management. Setting schedules, training others, interviewing, and showing leadership. You know regular manager duties. At nineteen years old, I would have been the youngest to ever hold that position.

Alisha: So why didn't you?

Ian: Life can be strange, sometimes for the bad, sometimes for good, and sometimes for the better.

Alisha: Okay, so what does that mean?

Ian: It means no, I didn't get it. I got something, maybe even better. I got the position I'm at now. So, here's how everything went. This is the history of Zip and where I come in Zip's history.

Erin: Another story time, yay!

Ian: So, Zip was founded back in 1987 by a young entrepreneur named Harrison Zip. He struggled at first, trying to get this new shipment company off the ground, especially during that time, when the competition was at an all-time high. You had other shipment companies who were already established and well known, as well as up and comers such as Zip themselves.

Alisha: What other delivery companies besides the big four?

Ian: Well, we know them as the big four today, which consists of Zip, of course. But we also have Postal, NBS or No Boundaries Services, and lastly, Orbiting Direct. Those are the big Four in the delivery slash receiving company that we see today. There were smaller companies just like Zip in '87, but throughout the years, one of the big four bought them out. Also, out of all the top companies I just named now, only Zip is not a government job. The rest of them are all backed by the government and have been since the year 2000. Mr. Zip saw an opportunity to increase revenue when the other big three were transitioning into government jobs.

Alisha: Why did the government back them? And why wasn't Zip backed by them? Or was that his choice?

Ian: I'm not sure why. I just know that's how it happened. The Big Three were now funded by the government, which made them the government. Zip has been independent and fighting to stay independent for years.

Erin: (confused by all this) What does indepen mean?

Ian: Not having to rely on anyone else. This is what the company Zip has been doing for over thirty years now. But wait, this is where I come in, girls. The story I'm going to share with you is the reason I believe Mr. Zip and his company Zip have been able to stay funded for so long and will continue to remain independent for a very long time. It all happened about ten years ago now. One day in the warehouse, another placer was arguing with a shifter over hours or his performance or something on those lines. Mr. Zip just got out of a meeting with some investors. So, he watches the entire argument take place between the two. He fired the placer personally for disrespecting his shifter. Later that evening, as Mr. Zip was leaving the building, he saw the placer he just fired in a truck, ready to run into this wall. I just finished my shift and was on the phone with Nicole talking about what would be for dinner. I noticed what was about to happen to Mr. Zip. Although it was getting dark, there was still some sunlight out, so I was able to dash over to him, still using my super strength. As soon as the placer put his foot on the gas, he went right towards Mr. Zip. But in the nick of time, I was able to jump in front of the truck and stop it with my bare hands, without hesitation. This was also like the first time I used my powers, too. The courier was injured because of the crash, but Mr. Zip was just in awe.

Erin: You stopped a truck? Cool!

Ian: Yeah. But right after that, I was embarrassed and afraid that I would get fired for not being "normal." Even doing the right thing sometimes can have you feeling bad about yourself.

Alisha: Was he at all thankful? What was his reaction?

Ian: Oh yes. He was thankful. He is grateful to be alive and to me for saving his life. Amazed at how quickly and how strong I was. He always wondered if there were people with powers out there like me. He used to read comics of heroes with supernatural abilities and gifts. He just thought it was so cool. So seeing that, with his own eyes, blew him away. He wouldn't stop thanking me.

Alisha: Did anyone else see it?

Ian: No. Like I said, the courier knocked himself out, and when workers came outside to see what happened, Mr. Zip told everyone that I tackled him out the way, and the courier ran into the wall. The courier was arrested.

Alisha: Did he give you a raise with that? I mean, you just saved his life, and all he can say is cool?

Ian: More than just that. So, for saving his life, he felt he owed me a debt he could never repay. He would forever be grateful; whatever I needed, he was there to help. He offered me a new job.

Alisha: What to be his bodyguard?

Ian: (laughing) Nah. He was starting a new branch for his company called ZAC, which stands for Zip Agency Codes. He offered me a job to be the top "Recruiter."

Alisha: I knew it! My Dad works for a secret society of assassins.

Ian: What? Where did you get that from? (Laughing) Anyway no. ZAC was a new elite Secret Service to help others in need around the world. So saving lives was mainly the job. Also, trying to prevent dangerous acts that can harm others was also part of the job. My job varies, but helping people or, let's say, being a service to people has been the calling for this branch. But no one knows about this part of Zip.

Alisha: How do you know who to help or where they are?

Ian: Mr. Zip is a rich wealthy man; he has his sources. He points at the map, and I go.

Alisha: All the time? That's a lot, Dad.

Ian: Well, when I'm not saving the world. I do recruit. Since Mr. Zip found out what I could do and my story growing up, he wanted to help those just like you and me, the ones who can't help themselves. So, I stay busy, and I go looking for dreamers too. Just like the other guy. Except, I'm helping and not hurting.

Erin: Don't you hurt people too?

Alisha: Dad is a hero, not a bad guy.

Ian: Sometimes, yes, I do have to harm people. Like I've said before, just the bad ones, Erin.

Alisha: Did you train doing all that, especially like at the diner? You were flipping and jumping high and could make a lot of different karate moves.

Ian: Yes. Mr. Zip invested in my training as well. I had to learn how to shoot and use a gun. I knew some karate already, but I got to learn more martial arts. I was even trained by ninjas.

Erin: Ninjas? That is too cool!

Ian: It was a cool experience, but it was hard. Hard, rigorous training. At times, I wanted to quit. I made it through, though. I kept thinking of your Mom, trying to make her proud. We were married by this time, and she was just pregnant with you, Alisha. So, me missing those times with her; I didn't want it to be all for nothing. So, I pushed myself until I made it through all my training and perfected it, too.

Alisha: Why would you need training anyway? You could just burn people away. You have the Sun's powers.

Ian: What if I ran into a problem like I had today? I would probably be dead by now, but I was prepared for any situation. That includes not having my powers. I still didn't fully understand my powers anyway. Still don't, honestly. But anything could have happened out there without my powers or that sun shining brightly.

Alisha: This is wild. All from saving a billionaire's life.

Ian: I think about it all the time, too. The reason I saved Mr. Zip was that he was in danger and was in need. Every so often it's right to do the right things and help others in need, not because you gain anything from it, but because it's just the right thing to do. So, Mr. Zip recognized that from me. It's like he could see in my heart that was still somewhat scarred; he has seen good in me, just like your mom and grandparents. So, I accepted after consulting your mom, of course also, after he agreed to my terms.

Alisha: What were your terms?

Ian: My terms were that regardless of what happens to me, my family or bloodline will always be held care of as long as Zip is a company, even when I'm long gone. When Mr. Zip is long gone. Even when you, Alisha, would be long gone. That we have his promise to be taken care of financially.

Alisha: Do you believe that?

Ian: I have to. Not having faith or worrying about someone not keeping their word is stressful. Sometimes there are good people with good intentions and with honest hearts, just like me. Flawed, but having a good heart, is more common than we sometimes think. I'm not saying trust every smile or every word people say. But you can't control what someone else will do or what they say. So, I chose wisely, but I learned to have trust in people because someone once trusted me.

Alisha: How did Mom take all this in?

Ian: She wasn't too sure about it at first. We just got married. Then she got pregnant with you when I went off for training. She supported my decision, and had a strong support system from her parents. She vowed never to tell anyone what I did and can do. She's kept her word, too. She never even told her parents, who were like her best friends, beside me. I always appreciated your mom for that.

Alisha: So why did you get so upset when she didn't speak to Brian about the Dream man?

Ian: Looking back at it, I might have overreacted. I just was worried about your safety. I know what he is capable of. Also, I didn't like being out of the loop; your mom actually was trying to do right by all of us. Once again, you two will see someday, but being a strong black woman isn't always easy. Your mom has done an excellent job of making it look easy.

Erin and Alisha smile at each other.

Alisha: Do you think some people you have "recruited" do you think they've seen Dream Man?

Ian: Yeah, I'm sure they have. Honestly, though, most people I recruit deny they have powers or gifts.

Alisha: Why?

Ian: Same reason you and I don't want people to know. They feel alone and uncertain of what happens next to them if they admit it, even though we want to help. We never use force or scare them. Force and scare are only for the bad guys. So, no pushbacks from us with people who don't wish to be helped, found or bothered.

Alisha: Have you ever failed a mission?

Ian: (silently thinking) Yes, I have.

Erin: What happened?

Ian: Well, to summarize. I was trying to save a family from some bad guys, breaking into a home, kind of ransom hostage situation. A father, mother, and their two children. Guns can be very dangerous, and they don't care who they harm; they just harm. So, I saved the father, mother and oldest daughter. I wasn't trying to kill any of them. I even spared all their lives, but one didn't care about that. He shot the youngest daughter. I still hear the cry, the mother screamed out, from that day. That was on me, not my team, but me. I always think of that little girl and what her life could have been. I don't like to talk about it or think about it. But, yeah. My first and last failed job.

Erin: Sorry.

Alisha: Yeah, sorry, Dad.

Ian: You girls are okay. I'll just leave it at that. Get some rest, okay?

Alisha: Yes, sir.

Ian: I'll wake you both in an hour. It's 2:17. I'll wake you up at 3:15.

CHAPTER 8

Sunshine

Thirty minutes pass by. Erin sits up.

Erin: Ian?

Ian: Oh, hey, Erin. Try to get some more sleep. You have another thirty minutes left before I'll wake you up.

Erin: Can't sleep.

Ian: I understand, but you need to get some rest.

Erin: Ok, but I'm scared.

Ian: Did you see the Dream Man?

Erin: No, but that Cowboy Man scared me. I was scared at the pizza diner when he started talking. Were you scared?

Ian: Yes and no.

Erin: Yes and no?

Ian: See, I wasn't scared to fight or hurt him because he was trying to hurt us. But the thought of losing crossed my mind for a second. I couldn't imagine what he would've done to you and your sister. Do you understand?

Erin: A little. Do you think Alisha was scared?

Ian: I believe Alisha is scared. She's on a journey to meet doctors who will run tests on her. They want to help, but the uncertainty, I'm sure, is bothering Alisha.

Erin: Is that what the Cowboy Man wanted to do?

Ian: I'm not sure what Walton wanted to do. But he has an agenda to hurt you both. And I have a job to protect you from people like him and the Dream Man.

Erin: Did you ever want to get rid of your powers?

Ian: When I was younger, yes. I've learned to appreciate it, though. I've learned to appreciate a lot in life.

Erin: Okay. Can I ask another question?

Ian: Okay, last one, then back to sleep.

Erin: Okay. Why do you call Alisha Sunshine? Did you have that nickname too?

Ian: Okay. So first, I call Alisha that because she has been the brightest part of my life since she was born. She also brightens up my heart when

I think of her. And no, no one ever called me sunshine. I was given a code name by Mr. Zip when I told him I had a living star inside of me.

Erin: Cool. What is your code name?

Ian: Sun Star. That's what I go by, out in the field. We don't use our real names, of course. So mine was Sun Star. Cool, huh?

Erin: So cool. So, When you have a star, does it hurt?

Ian: No, I sometimes forget it's there. I know my story from earlier may have been a lot for you to comprehend. But the sun gave me a smaller star that shines brightest when the sun is out. That's what brought out my super strength while fighting Walton. The only time I do feel pain is when it's dark or cloudy, or raining. My powers are very limited when the weather conditions are not in my favor.

Erin: So can you fly?

Ian: I don't think I can. Honestly, I don't know all that I can do besides enhancing my strength and speed. I never really thought more of it than that. I was just grateful for what I could do. I'm still learning, but I didn't think I ever needed to go further than that with my powers.

Erin: Why not?

Ian: I don't know, Erin. Like I said, never had to.

Erin: So you're not wasting your powers?

Ian: (confused) What do you mean? Waste my powers?

Erin: If I had the sun for powers, I would jump all the way up to the sun and talk to it.

Ian: That's physically impossible, Erin.(chuckling)

Erin: Have you tried it?

Ian: No.

Erin: Maybe you should. That would be so cool!

Ian: You know what, Erin, I think you were more excited about the fight than you were scared.

Erin: Yes, sir. You let that cowboy have it. I was scared, but I knew you would win.

Ian: (smiling) I sure did, didn't I. How did you know I would win, though?

Erin: You are the good guy. You are supposed to win.

Ian: We are the good guys! And hopefully, we always win. He will be back, though. So just be prepared.

Erin: Okay.

Ian: Let me ask you something. What powers would you want when you get them?

Erin: (staring out the window) I would want to put people's lives back together when they fall apart. Sort of like a…puzzle. I love puzzles.

Ian: That actually wouldn't be too bad of a power.

Erin: I would put you and my mom in a happier place.

Ian: (confused) Don't you mean your mom and your dad. Your mother and I aren't married anymore.

Erin: Yeah, I know. But I feel that I'm the reason you, Mom, and Alisha aren't a family anymore.

Ian: Erin. Your mother made a mistake. A very big mistake. But your mother isn't a bad woman. I made mistakes too, but I'm not a bad man either. Sometimes people have relationships that grow apart, and it's for the better. You are the reason that your mom and dad have a beautiful family, along with your sister. That's how it should be. And I'm just happy that Alisha, you, and Nicole are all happy. And that's what Brian does for you all. Do you understand?

Erin: I understand. Thank you, Mr. I.

Ian: You're welcome, Little E.

Erin: Are you going to kill Walton and Dream Man?

Ian: (Pauses for a second) It's a possibility that that might be my only option. If I need to protect you girls, then yes, I will.

Erin: Is that why you got your code name? You can kill people just like the sun. My Dad says the sun can hurt you or even kill you.

Ian: It most certainly can. So, That's one way you can look at it. But I was given the name because of my skin too. When the sun hits my skin at the right angle, it's like I shine brighter. Also, I have a killer smile that can blind you. (Laughing) But that's the main reason. The sun doesn't affect me like it does to others. It's a power source for me, and unless that sun is turned off, I'm the strongest on this planet.

Erin: So you actually have superpowers? Which means that you are a hero?

Ian: Far from a hero, but if you were to call me one, call me an Enhanced Hero. Without that sun, though, I'm just your average Joe.

Erin: If you say so.

Ian: Go to sleep, Little E. Get some rest.

As they arrive in Minnesota, Ian, and the girl's pullover at the public mall.

Alisha: Why are we stopping here?

Ian: I need to make a phone call here. We are finally in Minnesota, but we are outside of St. Cloud. I need to call you guy's uncle to get the exact address.

Alisha: What are you going to use, a pay phone? That's what it is called, right? Or is that too old school?

Ian: No, I'm going to be using my phone. My untraceable, untracked phone. The only way someone could pick up a signal is if I'm on the phone too long and a camera picks up the signal.

Alisha: What? How fair is that? You can use a phone, but mine can get taken away. You said no phones.

Ian: I know what I said. That's why I haven't used it until now. It's more like an electronic device that so happens to call people. Now be quiet. Let me make this phone call. Then we can find a restroom for you girls in the mall.

Alisha: Dad, which mall is this?

Ian: Just a mall. Not Mall of America, and no, we can't go shopping.

Alisha: I don't think we will have time for that. But I don't think we should stop here? Can we go somewhere else?

Ian pulls his electric device out and scans the mall for their entrances, their bathrooms, and for anyone with guns inside. He finds nothing that can be a threat to them. He looks through his contacts and finds the facility number. Calls the facility, dials Will's extension line.

Ian: Why do you want to go somewhere else? You still haven't been truthful with me, Alisha. You seem worried too. I understand being afraid of these guys. But it seems to come and go with you and Erin, now that I think of it. What aren't you telling me?

Alisha: Just forget I said anything. Let's play patty cake, Erin.

Erin: I love patty cake.

Ian: Alisha! I heard you and your mother whispering last night as I was leaving out. She asked whether you saw it like that. Then you don't know the highway, but then you know it suddenly. Then you said something about the diner, and Walton showed up because he was tracking us. Also, you almost knew what Walton, and I were going to do with our moves; how?

The device is still calling Will.

Alisha: Lucky guess, dad.

Ian: No, Alisha. You girls have shown a lot of courage, too, too much courage. Why don't you want to go inside this mall?

Will finally pick's up. Ian notices Will is breathing heavily.

Will: (whispering) Hello? Hello?

Ian: Hello, is this Will?

Will: Yes, yes, it is. (trying to catch his breath)

Ian: Hey, wasup man, this is Ian, Alisha's Dad. Just crossed to Minnesota. Maybe another hour or so before we make it to Wolves Den. Damn, bruh, everything okay over there?

Will: Um, can the girls hear me? (still struggling to catch his breath)

Ian: Nah, you cool, man. Is everything alright?

Will: Not exactly, we had some unexpected visitors. It's a guy with a black coat, claiming to be the owner of our company, and asking for the girls.

Ian: Owner of the company? It must be Walton. We ran into him a few hours ago. Does he look like a cowboy and missing a right arm?

Will: No, this one is no one near that description. He's tall, has a black coat and is very frightening.

Ian: Wait, is he sort of moving like a shadow?

Will: Like a shadow? Nah, man. He's definitely moving, though. Moving pretty fast, too. We asked what his business was, and he told us that he would wait for you and the girls.

Ian: Did he say his name? Did he know the girl's name specifically?

Will: Never gave us his name, but he knew the girl's names and yours too.

Ian: Will, what does DOP stand for?

Will: It stands for Dreams Of Powers.

Ian: Dreams Of Powers. How long have you guys been "helping people" or seen people with powers? Don't lie either. I don't care about that consent you probably signed.

Will: What does that have to do-

Ian: Answer the question! How long?

Will: I'm not sure, man. It's been around for a while. The very least 100 years.

Ian: He's been around that long?

Will: The guy who's here now? Do you think he really is the owner?

Ian: He has to be, and you guys have been unknowingly helping him get these powers.

Will: So one doctor asked what he needed them for, and he um...

Ian: Say no more. I know where this is going. He killed him, didn't he?

Will: Yeah... and he was a great doctor too. He did it with no remorse, too. That doctor had a wife and kids, man. We all are a little afraid. But I won't give you and the girls up; they're going to have to kill me to get any answers about my nieces. He hasn't found me yet. And after what they did to my brother. I don't know how much longer I have, man.

Ian: (shocked) Woah! What? What did they do? What do you mean?

Will: You don't know? When's the last time you spoke with Nicole? Hasn't she called or texted you?

Ian: She was texting Alisha earlier, but that gave our whereabouts away from the cowboy guy I mentioned earlier. I haven't talked with them since we left this morning. Last I heard, they were heading to her parents, and I was going to call when we made it to the facility. What happened Will?

Will: Um.

Ian: Will I need you to tell me what happened. Did they hurt Nicole, Brian, or her parents? (whispering)

Will: I've been trying not to think about it. But Yeah, man. Nicole and Brian never made it to her parents' house. This Dream guy killed my brother.

Ian is stunned.

Will: Hello (whispering). Are you still there?

Ian: Yeah. Look, Will, man, I'm sorry. I had no idea. How….. How do you know?

Will: The Dream man showed it to us. Trying to draw me out. He killed a few more people. That's when everyone scattered out of there. It is not safe to bring the girls here, man.

Ian: So where do we go now?

Will: I don't know. Somewhere far from here. I'm going to have to confront this Dream guy soon. So, no one else gets hurt or killed. These dudes aren't playing. These dudes killed my brother, man. It's replaying in my head now. I can't seem to stop thinking about tha-

(Ian hears the henchman in the background.)

Henchman: There you are. Get back here!

Will: You need to call to check on Nicole, man! I gotta go.

Ian: (still in disbelief) Okay!

Alisha and Erin, looking back at Ian, noticed a concerned look.

Alisha: Dad? What's wrong? What happened?

Ian begins to call Nicole. A truck pulls up beside their truck.

Walton: Howdy! Grab the girls!

Walton shoots Lela's tires out.

Ian: Get out!

Alisha: Is that them?

Ian: Get out now! We need to get another car now. This won't make it.

Alisha: Do we have time?

Ian: Alisha! Shut up and do what I say. Now is not the time to ask argue.

Ian grabs two bulletproof vests. He grabs his gun and begins to shoot at Walton.

Ian: Erin, put this bulletproof vest on! Alisha, take this one and put it on. Hurry up, stand behind me and make sure your sister has hers on too. I'll try to hold them off.

Alisha: Dad, where's yours?

Ian: I only have two. (continues to shoot at Walton) I'll be fine as long as I don't get shot. Erin needs mine, and I can't take yours. You haven't been healing properly, so I don't want to take that risk with you.

Alisha and Erin look at each other, they hesitantly put the vests on.

Alisha: Daddy, there's something I need to tell you…

Ian: Not now, Alis--

Walton shoots some more

Walton: Haw! Told you I'd be back!

Ian: Get inside now!

Ian and the girls maneuver through cars heading into the mall. Walton and his men continue to shoot. Some pedestrians get hit in the crossfire as some begin to run away from the shooting. Ian and the girls made it into the mall. They run through a clothing store. Walton is in no rush; he devises a plan. Thinking about sacrificing a few men in the process.

Walton: (talking with his men, missing his right arm) You two go after them through the clothing store.

Two henchmen follow Ian and the girls into the clothing store.

Walton: You three, come with me. The rest of you all go to the front entrance. Call "Him" and let "him" know this will be over soon. Have "him" meet us at the front entrance. It Shouldn't take "him" long to get here; it might actually take a few minutes. This is a final standoff, gentleman. Do your job, kill whoever gets in the way, and don't let them get away. Or there will be consequences for all of us.

Ian, Alisha, and Erin are still running through the clothing store; as they are about to reach the outside of the clothing store, Walton's two henchmen catch up with them.

The first henchman grabs Ian on his right shoulder, turning him around. The second henchman grabs Erin and Alisha.

Alisha: Let go of us!

While the first henchman is holding Ian's shirt by the shoulder, Ian quickly grabs the henchman's right arm and swings him into a rack of clothes, crashing into the rack. Ian then rushes to the second henchman with a flying right knee to the chest, sending him crashing into a mirror. Ian takes the girls back, and they begin to run.

Alisha: Where did Walton and the others go? It looks like it was just them two.

Ian: Not sure, but we need to keep running before the catch-up.

They run out of the store, and a third henchman hits Ian on the right side of his face. As Ian stumbles to his left, he knocks Erin and Alisha to the ground. The third henchman goes for another punch, but is countered with a rolling arm lock by Ian. Ian proceeds to break the third henchman's arm on the ground after the roll-up. The second henchman is seen upside from Ian's viewpoint, and he tries to stomp on Ian's head with his right foot. But Ian rolls underneath him, grabbing his left foot while getting up. Ian turns the henchman around to face him, punches the henchman's face, breaking his nose, and then flips him on the top of his head onto the floor, having the mall deafened by the thud noise of the henchman's head.

Alisha: Dad! (Alisha and Erin being dragged away by the first henchman)

Ian runs towards the henchman and tackles him over the balcony from the second floor. The henchman lets go of the girls and yell on his way down from the second floor. Ian holds onto the henchman's collar with both hands, with his left knee pushed against the henchman's torso. The henchman falls back first to the first floor. As he falls, Ian does a forward roll. As Ian cachets his balance, Alisha and Erin run down the escalator.

Alisha: Oh my goodness, Dad, are you alright?

Ian: Ye. Yeah, I'm okay. No time for a breather. We have to keep moving. Let's head to the front parking lot; it's up ahead of us to our left.

Ian and the girls continue running in the mall as they hit the left around the corner. They finally run back into Walton and the rest of his men.

Alisha: This guy again?

Erin: Just leave us alone!

Walton: Can't do that; this "protector" of yours just killed two more of my men. Broke one of my men's arm. You also took my right arm. There are going to be consequences for all of this.

Ian: None of that is my fault. I have no choice but to protect these girls. I have a duty and a responsibility to keep these girls safe at all costs. Unfortunately for you and your men, I still have a job to do.

Walton: So you should understand Ian better than anyone about a job or, let's call it, a mission. To be quite honest with you, this is just like another mission for you, huh?

Ian: No, don't do that either.

Walton: Don't do what? Oh, I see, so this isn't just like your missions. This is what you do, right? Help others? Save others? No matter the casualties or the innocent people caught in the crossfire. Like those people back in the diner. They all died. I made sure of it, too, when you guys left.

Alisha: You killed all those people? All of those innocent people?

Walton: Yeah, I had a "job" to do. I have responsibilities, and we are no different from your father. See also; your father left those people to die. Innocent people too, who didn't deserve that. They loved pizza, arcade games, and beer.

Alisha: So why did you kill them?

Walton: That goes back to I have a job to do, just like your father. Your father could have called someone or helped those people out. A life could have been saved. But no, your dad has a mission to accomplish. We all have assignments and priorities, and your father is not so different from us "bad guys."

Ian: That is totally different from what you are doing.

Walton has his men circle Ian and the girls.

Walton: How Ian? The people you hurt or kill have families, and they go home to someone, too, right? You are not the hero that you want these girls to believe. You're not even the hero you believe to be. You are an angry, hurt individual who finds peace by inflicting pain on others, since you were never able to as a kid.

Ian: That's not true! You know nothing about me.

Walton: Clearly, I do. Clearly, "He" does. He's told me all about you. Hey, Alisha. You might have been thinking your dad is some great hero, helping people, saving the world, making it a better place. Come on, look what your Dad was capable of doing just a second ago. He killed two men, and one's up there with his arm broken, screaming for help as we speak.

Alisha: You are trying to hurt us. He's trying to protect us from people like you. And the Dream man!

Walton: You believe that too, don't you, little girl. That your dad is doing this for you. Your father barely knows you. I mean, think about it, he's been on the road since you were born. Leaving your mother to raise you all this time. He isn't the man he thinks he is, and he's damn sure not the father you want to believe he is. Oh, and Erin, this little mission is just that. You and your sister are just missions. Or let's say another accomplishment or milestone that Ian has reached for self-validation.

Erin and Alisha look over to see Ian's face.

Alisha: Is that true, daddy? Are we just another mission? You know who I am, right?

Walton: Sure, he knows who you are, the person. But he doesn't know who you are as a person, little miss sunshine. I'm sure you two have even bonded about having some powers together, right? Oh, that's right, you two haven't because you don't want them. And he "knows" what's best for you, right? You two have something in common for once to bond over; beforehand, not much interest. Damn shame, Ian.

Ian: Don't listen to him, girls (still staring at Walton). He's trying to tear us apart.

Walton: No, Ian, that's something you've done already because you were out "saving the world." Alisha, Erin, come with me, and the Dream man can truly help you two. Alisha, you don't want those powers anymore. Step to me, and he will get you that normal life you desire. The one that your father has always wanted to have, but messed that all up for himself. Look, my boss has arrived and is outside right now. I can't go out there empty-handed. And he's on a time schedule.

Ian: They are going nowhere with you. Nowhere with "Him." And definitely not with any of your stooges. If that means killing all of you in front of everyone in this mall. Then I will do that. I am willing to go to great lengths for these girls, as I have before. Sacrifice my eyes now, so they can cry of joy later. Put my body on the line today, so they can rest theirs for tomorrow. I am prepared to counter all of those lies you just told to make sure my truth hits ten times harder. Are you prepared to lose round two, Walton?

Walton: You think it will be that easy, huh?

Ian: Nah! But I know I'll come out the winner, regardless.

Walton: So confident. Man, that's your most likeable trait.

Ian: Then you will love this!

Ian shoots his gun, but Walton evades the bullets with some neck movements.

Walton: My turn!

Walton quickly draws his.44 and shoots Ian in his left shoulder and right chest.

Ian: Uhh! (falling onto his back)

Alisha: Daddy!

Walton: Join him!

Walton then shoots Alisha on her left side.

Alisha: Ahhh! (falling to her back)

Ian and Alisha begin to bleed out.

Erin: Ahhhh! Alisha!

Walton: Take the girl. She's going to bleed out, but we don't need her. I'm taking my losses on with her.

(The henchman picks up Erin and leaves Alisha.)

Erin: (screaming and yelling at the top of her lungs.) NO! Mr. I! Don't let them take me, please!!

Walton: Shut up, girl!

Ian is now bleeding out. He looks over at Alisha, bleeding out next to him. He looks up at the ceiling. He sees the Sun is now shining bright, right above him. It's a couple of feet from his head.

Ian: (whispering to himself) Alisha.

With his head back, Ian begins to have regrets and thoughts about what could have been.

Ian: (Thinking to himself) How did I let this happen? Is this it? For all of us. Did I just let Alisha and Erin down? Am I about to lose them both? Am I going to die? I don't have the strength to go directly underneath that sunlight. I need it, though. God, not like this! I'm begging for something to happen.

Erin: Ian! Ian! Alisha! Alisha! ALISHA!!(reaching out to them both)

As Erin is reaching out. Ian feels a sharp piercing coming through his left shoulder and the right side of his chest.

Ian: (yelling in pain. Thinking to himself) What is this God awful pain? I've been shot before, but this is different.

The bullet fragments begin to form back together inside Ian's shoulder and chest. He feels every bit flowing through his body. Ian looks over at Alisha. Her eyes are wide open, and she's screaming in agony now. The blood that was just oozing out from her left side is now being vacuumed back inside her side.

Alisha: Ahhh! Ahh!

Ian's head lays back down. He sees the clouds moving south again, blocking the little bit of sunlight in the sky roof again.

Ian (thinking to himself) What is happening? Something doesn't feel right. I can't make out what Erin is trying to say. Ian tries to lift his head up, but realizes something else is developing. He isn't controlling his movements. He's watching Walton walk backward with Erin. He hears Erin speaking strangely. Sounds like she was speaking another language. He then understands she's talking backward. Everything is reversing.

Ian: How is this happening? What is happening?

Walton sets Erin back down. His men backup and form that circle again. Erin lays her head and hands on Alisha's chest.

Erin: Alisha! (weeping)

Then Erin rises up and then watches Alisha instantly get back up. The bullet flies out of Alisha. Ian then instantly stands back up, and both bullets fly out of his body. Ian's arm raises back up, and he feels the bullet he shot at Walton come right back to his gun. Walton is back where he was, too.

Everything is now back in place before Ian shot at Walton.

Walton: What the hell just happened? How the hell did you do that, Ian?

Ian: That wasn't me! I know now what's really going on here.

Ian takes his eyes off Walton and looks at the girls. Alisha is shocked. Erin has her head down, crying.

Walton: Men! I see now (With a grin on his face)

Ian: So do I! I just saw what happens next.

Walton pulls his.44 back out and points it at the girls. Ian wraps his arms around them. But Walton fakes him out. Stretches his arms out and grabs the back of Ian's shirt. Walton flings Ian toward him. As Ian is coming back toward Walton, he looks up to see where the sun is. He reaches to Walton.

Walton: (holding Ian) She just moved back in time! That's why he wants her!

Walton takes his 44 and shoots Ian in his chest, sending him a few feet away from behind him. Walton turns back around to the girls.

Walton: We need both of them now! Grab them!

Alisha: Daddy! Daddy! Erin, can you do it again! Erin, do it again! Please, Erin, try to do it again! Daddy!

Erin: I can't! (crying) I'm sorry, Alisha, I can't!

Ian: Ahh!!

Ian looks back into the sky; he feels himself fading away. He then feels some heat on the side of his face. He looks up and sees he's underneath one of the sky roof openings. The sun is now shining bright. Ian mustards up enough strength and scoots himself back just enough.

Ian: (telling himself) C'mon, Ian. You got enough in you. C'mon Ian. Keep fighting, Ian. Keep going. Just a little bit more.

Ian finally has his body underneath the entire Sky opening. His eyes close. And he believes this is the end!

Walton: Stop crying for your daddy. He's gone! Sorry to do that to you, girls. But we got somewhere to be.

Alisha: Daddy!

Erin: Big I! Please! Wake up! I'm sorry! Please wake up.

Ian hears this. Something in him tells him. "It's Time!"

He begins to feel this ball of energy within. His heart aches, and he feels little star begin to burn in his chest. He closes his eyes and can feel the star burning from inside all over his body. He then wakes up with fire in both eyes.

CHAPTER 9

Trust

Flashback to Walton in 1901. He's an outlaw being chased by some bounty hunters in the Nevada mountains. As he's riding his horse, Walton sees a man in a black coat from a distance. Walton draws his gun out to shoot him, but Walton is pushed off his horse when he tries to pass the mysterious man up.

Walton: What the hell! (falling from his horse. As he gets up, he pulls his gun out) You just made a grave mistake as soon as I'm done with these bounty hunters. I'll deal with you!

Unknown Stranger: I don't make mistakes! I know exactly what I'm doing. Take a good look at me; you might recognize who I am if you do.

Walton: Wait! Are you him? I haven't seen you in about forty years. You're the man from my dreams! The Dream Man. What are you doing here? Why are you here?

Dream Man: Yes, that's right. I'm the Man in from dreams. I have been watching you, Walton. Now get out of the way. I will take care of these bounty hunters.

Walton: Look, man, I'm worth a lot of money. These guys won't stop until I'm caught. Unless you are working with them? Is that what this is? Are you here for my bounty, too?

The bounty hunters reach Walton and Dream Man.

Bounty hunter 1: Well, this seems like the end for you, Walton Ross. Not sure who this fella is with you. If he's a man who's in your crew, the better. Unless he's Hunter himself, so who are you, feller?

Dream Man: That's not it at all. I am here for Walton. I don't care for the money! This is a loss you guys might want to just accept. This won't end well for any of you.

The bounty hunters all laugh.

Bounty Hunter 1: That's a threat in my books, boys! What do y'all think?

They all agree with a nod.

Dream Man: Well, let's settle this like men. One of you up for a challenge?

Bounty Hunter 1: A challenge today. Walton, you might want to get your boy!

Walton: (looking at the Dream Man) You have no piece! Are you crazy? Let me duel him. I'm the faster man in the West; he knows it, too. Don't you Steve?

Steve: Nah, now, I was challenged by him, and I accept his challenge. Walton Ross, you might as well lasso yourself. He also doesn't have a gun either. Lend him yours, Walton.

Dream man: I'm fine without it. Get off that horse and accept your fate.

Steve jumps off his horse

Steve: On the count of three. My count!

Dream man: Fine by me.

Steve: One.

Walton: You need a gun, man. You gonna get us both killed here!

Steve: Two!

Dream Man quickly throws a knife into Steve's chest.

Steve: Uhh. (Looking down at the knife through his chest)

Walton: What? When did you?

The other bounty hunters with a confused look on their faces. Watch as Steve falls back, smacking the ground, dying instantly.

Bounty Hunter Two: Shoot them sons of bit-

Flick! Bounty Hunter Two looks down at his chest. The rest of the crew stare in fear. One of them finally shoots, but is also met with a throwing knife.

Dream man begins to throw all his knives in many directions. Flick! Flick! Flick! Flick!

Walton: (Amazed and speechless) How? When?

Dream Man: How, when, what?

Walton: I'm the quickest in the west, and I couldn't even see you throw those knives? How did you get so quick? And why are you here? How did you even find me? Should I just lasso myself? I can't defeat you. Who uses knives anyway? You threw them with no problem.

Dream Man: No, Walton. I'm here for you. I've been watching you for a very longtime now. You missed out on your powers; sorry for that.

Walton: Powers? I have power! I'm just on the run for right now.

Dream Man: Oh, so you have power, huh? Well, can your type of power do this?

Grabbing Walton, Dream Man leaps off the mountains, down onto train tracks.

Walton: What? How did we? Where are we… is that a train?

A train, coming full speed, sounds it's horn and bell at Walton and Dream Man.

Dream Man: Don't move!

Walton: (Yelling) Ahh!

The Dream Man runs towards the train, but the train splits in half when they collide. Coal and Gold start spilling out.

Walton: (In disbelief again) How? What are you?

Dream Man: This is power. Take that gold there. Get your name cleared. You're a rich man now. I'll be seeing you again someday.

Walton: You're not going to show me or teach me how to do any of those things?

Dream Man: Just be ready when I come to see you again. Trust me.

Walton pays his bounty fees, along with his gang's bounties, too.

Eighteen years later, Walton is now in his sixties and is very wealthy. The Dream Man pays Walton a visit to his home in Nevada. Some of Walton's gang now are his bodyguards.

As Dream Man walks, he is greeted by Walton with a handshake.

Walton: It's been a long time. I thought you'd never be back.

Dream Man: Told you I would. Now I got something for you. But I'm also going to need something from you first.

Walton: I don't really need anything else anymore. I'm wealthy, thanks to you, of course. I'm very powerful now.

Dream Man: Do I need to demonstrate true power again? This is true power. Go to sleep.

Walton: No need to demonstrate. I feel more alive and haven't been tired in a long. This is also my home. Be a guest, relax, and grab a drink.

Dream Man: I don't think you remember what power is. Let me show you, Walton.

Some of Walton's goons unclip their gun holsters.

Dream Man: Oh, unless these guys are not your most loyal gang members, tell them to stand down. Unless they want to end up like those bounty hunters from years ago.

Walton: It's alright, boys. He's cool. He's the reason we all cleared our names.

Dream Man: Thank you for your acknowledgment. Now give me your gun, Walton.

Walton hands him his.44.

Walton: You're not going to kill us, are you?

Dream Man grabs the gun.

Dream Man: No. Just building trust. (Checking to see how many bullets are in the barrel) And every building. (Closes the barrel) Needs a foundation!

Dream Man raises the gun and points it toward Walton.

Walton: Wait! You said you-

Bang! Bang! Bang! Bang! Bang! Bang! Bang!

With his hands up, Walton sees that he's now standing behind Dream Man. He checks to see if he was shot at all and feels no bullet wounds. Dream Man turns and looks at Walton, opens Walton's hands, and drops the bullets into Walton's hands.

Dream Man: This is the foundation of our trust. This is the second time and the fourth power of mine that I've shown you.

Walton: I don't even know what you just did or what just happened.

Dream Man: Just as I saved you from those bounty hunters, I've shown you speed and agility. When I split that train into two and gave you that gold, that was the power of strength. So now, eighteen years later, you and I have both shown a new power that we can sort of manipulate or bend to our advantage. That power is trust.

Walton: Trust? I trust you. But how did I show you any trust? How is that a power too? That's character.

Dream Man: True it is, but we use it as a tool or as a weapon. That's how I've gotten so powerful, through trusting and believing. Taken what I want, but these powers that I have, I've used to good work. And I trust you now because you've shown your allegiance to your gang. Not only did you get yourself out of debt, but you pulled your gang with you.

Walton: Never leave a man behind!

Dream Man: Perfect, that's what I like to hear. Because you all work for me now, this is where our foundation of trust builds into a house of strength. A powerhouse. I want more power, and we desire more power.

Walton: What do you mean "work" for you? More power, how? We have all the money we could need. We don't need to rob banks anymore or put fear into our enemies. Going town to town, risking our lives for that. We're old men now.

Dream Man: Not as old as me. And believe me, you guys will live for a long time working for me. And I say working for me because you owe a debt to me. This life that you have today is because of me. Always remember that. Always trust and believe my words.

Walton: Owe you a debt, huh? When do I pay this debt off?

Dream Man: How much money have you spent? How much gold have you used? A lot, I take it. That's the debt. And I trust you will follow my lead in the era of power. And as we continue to grow this house.

Walton: What are these jobs we have to do? I'm a cowboy; not much I can do with just guns, especially if we are going to run into people like you.

Dream Man: Like us. I told you, I trust you. Enough trust that I believe you deserve powers, too. Oh! And the jobs. You will just have one title. Walton Ross, the Bounty Hunter. Hunter for powers!

Walton: A bounty Hunter. Ok. Here that boys? We gonna be doing the chasing around here now!

Dream Man: Yes! Now sleep.

Walton: Not too sleepy, though. Any advice.

Dream Man: Yeah, get blackout drunk as usual. I'll see you soon.

Walton goes to sleep. He opens his eyes, but to the pitch black.

Walton: Hello? Anyone here?

Walton sees a shadowy figure approaching him. Dream Man emerges from the shadow.

Walton: So, will I be able to do that?

Dream Man: You can do just about whatever; in a dream. No one, though, can do what I do! I have a lot of supernatural powers. Some skills I might not use as much anymore, but nonetheless, I have them.

Walton: How did you become so powerful?

Dream Man: By taking others' abilities and gifts through their dreams. Just like you would take from others, rob others, hurt others to get what you need. Same here. I see the best and worst in people while they are dreaming. That's how I found you.

Walton: I was a wild one at that time when I first saw you.

Dream Man: That I know, but with guidance, I feel that you have the potential to be great. Having even more power than what you have now.

Walton: So, are we going to stand in your shadow, or am I going to get my powers?

Dream Man: (smirking) I just knew you were going to be the best man for this. Let's take a dive.

Walton: A dive? Dive where? We have nowhere to-

Dream Man tilts Walton's head forward a bit, and they teleport outside.

Walton: What? We were just up the-

Dream Man takes Walton's head and tilts him forward again. They are now standing in front of their home.

Walton: Please don't do that again. Where are we?

Dream Man: Little Rock, Arkansas. This home belongs to the Pin family. Husband, wife and their two kids stay in this home. The first child is a boy with no gifts or powers. But the second child is a girl. And man, she has unbelievable power.

Walton: What can she do? And can anyone see us?

Dream Man: We are in a dream. Actually, we are in this little girl's dream. Her name is Jen. And she can stretch her limbs away from her body.

Walton: Stretch her body?

Dream Man: Yes, about 15 feet away from the rest of her body. If she continues to practice, or if I continue to teach her, she'll be able to stretch her limbs about sixty feet from her body by the time she's hit her twenties.

Walton: Yeah, but you can teach me how to do that, right?

Dream Man: No, I can't do that. What I can do is take that power away from her and give it to you.

Walton: And how would you do that?

Dream Man: Well, that would mean we would have to keep her in this dream. I've been befriending her or making her think I'm her friend. Showing her how to use this gift. She lets her guard down with me. She trusts me. That gives us the opportunity to take her power.

Walton: I got that part, but what happens to her?

Dream Man: You were an outlaw once before; you know how these things go. When you are robbing someone, usually there are casualties involved. So, unfortunately, she will not live after we take her powers.

Walton: (thinking) So she will die? By just taking her powers? Why can't we take them without killing her or hurting her?

Dream Man: Believe me, if I could, I would. There is no other way. These gifts and abilities are one with people. It's like an organ that functions in the body and keeps you alive. You don't realize it's there until you learn about it. Most don't even know they have these powers. Let alone know how to function without them.

Walton: So you want to give me her powers? Killing her. All for what? You said you want me to be like those bounty hunters that were after me when you and I first ran into each other. Except I'll be chasing down people with abilities like you to bring to you so you can gain more power. Why do I get the feeling that this only benefits you?

Dream Man: Not just me who benefits from this. Us! Sure, I have strength unimaginable. I can fly and move fast. But I'm only one man. I can't be everywhere or every place when I need to be. And I'm at my strongest in dreams. So while I'm getting the powers for us, you will find them and hold them until I get to them.

Walton: Kids? We are hunting kids!

Dream Man: Not just kids. Man, you make me sound like a monster. Anyone with abilities that aren't using them is actually beneficial for our quest for power. Kids are just less aware of the danger. I know it sounds unethical, but that's the price for this. Price for power.

Walton: I didn't know your powers were built off the blood of others like this, especially children. This is not sitting well with me.

Dream Man: When you were an outlaw, a lot of your money came at the expense of others, too, right? Look at it this way. You might not feel good about it at first, but think of your gang and crew you have been running with. Think of their families and the generations after them. They will benefit from this as well, as they have already through your wealth. If there's one thing I know too, you don't want your crew to go without.

Walton: So will they be getting them powers too?

Dream Man: (nodding) Of course they would. I want a team. People that I can trust and help us achieve this goal for power. All of us will benefit from this.

Walton thinking.

Dream Man: Also, remember you owe me this, too. If you don't want to do this, that's fine, and I understand. But with that being said, I will take back all the wealth I've given you. Then you can tell your crew it's all gone. I will find another with as much potential and not second-guessing themselves in their later years. Let's head back!

Walton: Wait! I'm just trying to wrap my head around all of this. I want t-

Jen: Hey, Mister friend! I didn't think you were coming today.

Dream Man: Hi, Jen. This is our new friend Walton. He's a nice man, like me. He wants to be your friend too.

Walton looks over at the Dream Man. Walton waves reluctantly.

Walton: Hey there, Jen.

Jen: Hi! Are you going to learn with us today, too?

Dream Man: No, he's about to be leaving.

Walton: It was nice to meet you, Jen.

Jen: You too! Hope to see you again.

Dream Man walks, Walton away.

Dream Man: I'm going to send you back to our world. This won't take long. When you wake up, you'll have real powers.

As Dream Man holds Walton's head to tilt him back, Walton looks on and sees Jen.

Back to the present day. Walton is leaving with a screaming, upset Erin. Some other men are dragging Alisha.

Alisha: Erin, do it again! You have to try.

Erin: (crying) I can't, Alisha! I don't know how.

Ian raises up to his feet, with star fire burning in his eyes.

Alisha: Dad? (sniffling and wiping her nose)

Ian leaps up and tears part of the ceiling away. More sunlight shines into the mall. The sunlight powers Ian up more, allowing him to float in the air. His strength increases, as does his anger.

Ian: Bring them back!

Walton becomes confused and shocked. As Ian is floating, he drops hard to the ground, landing on his hands and left knee.

BOOM! Cracking, then breaking the surface beneath him. Knocking back Walton's goons, who are still circled around Alisha and Erin.

Walton: (Widened eyes) How? You should be dead! This isn't a normal power.

Walking towards Walton and the girls. Walton walks backwards, slowly and cautiously.

Ian: I told you to leave us alone. I told you I wouldn't be so generous this time. I told you those things, didn't I?

Walton: You did. But c'mon feller, what did you expect?

Ian: To be left alone!

Walton extends his left arm out to grab Ian. Ian catches his arm, burning Walton's knuckles.

Walton: Ahhhh!! (Walton drops to his knees and starts to feel and see the skin of his knuckles burning off.)

Ian changes back to his regular form.

Ian: Girls! Get over here now!

Alisha and Erin run over to Ian as quickly.

Ian: Stay behind me and don't touch me!

Walton: My hand! What did you do to me? What are you?

Ian: What should've been done earlier. Once again, I told you to leave us alone. Now that I have you at my mercy, tell me everything about the Dream Man!

Walton: What? I don't even know much about him!

Ian: You don't know much about the man you work for? So, you just go around catching and helping him hurt these kids? If you can't give me anything, you're no use to me.

Walton: Ok. Ok. Ok!

Ian: Why does he want Alisha and Erin? Besides their powers. Why send you for them? And don't give me, "that's my job, bs."

Walton: We just witnessed what that little one can do. We should be at the facility by now, had she not rewind things like that!

Ian: (Turning to Erin) That was you? You are the one that can heal?

Walton: Who else would've it been? You can't be that out of touch with them. You really don't know what's going on, huh?

Ian is visibly upset.

Ian: Shut up! (turning to Walton, then back to Erin.) Erin, was that you?

Erin: (head down) No, sir. I can't heal.

Ian: Alisha? What is really going on? We should be dead right now! Please tell me you healed us. Please tell me I'm not tripping and being lied to, even at this very moment.

Alisha: Erin didn't heal you, daddy. (lowering her head.)

Ian: Ok. So if you didn't heal us, Alisha? And you didn't either, Erin? What just happened?

Alisha: Daddy. I'm sorry I've been lying to you. The truth is, I can't heal, but I seem to know how everything plays out. I couldn't see past our deaths, though. You and I die here, so I didn't want to go into the mall. We never made it to Uncle Will. And Erin is dragged away. We didn't want to tell you because we knew you would try to avoid it.

Ian: How would you know I would avoid it? We could have gone another way. And did your mom know all of this would happen, too?

Alisha: (head down) No. she didn't know this would happen. I have seen so many different times on so many different routes that we took. You and I die, and Erin is carried away by Dream Man.

Ian: Did you see this in your dream? Is that your actual power?

Alisha: Yes. I guess that's what my powers will really be. I never met the Dream man; we made up the entire story, so you can help take Erin to the facility for protection and possibly get rid of her powers altogether. Uncle Will said that they might actually have the machine and antidotes to do that.

Ian: It still doesn't explain how we are still alive.

Alisha: That was Erin. Dad, Erin can rewind time. She might be able to time travel too.

Ian: She can what?

Alisha: We saw her do it before when she got upset with me. She kept talking about her imaginary friend in her dreams that she saw every day. That would come to visit her. We all thought she was just talking until finally, I told her he was real, and if he were, he wouldn't be her friend. I was teasing her and playing around with her. That's when it happened. Mom, Brian, and I all saw her get angry and rage. Just kind of like you did just a second ago. And just like she did moments ago.

Ian: How did it play out?

Erin: I didn't like her talking about my friend like that. Or I thought he was my friend. I just moved my arm out like this(reaching her arm out) and just pushed the air. We just moved backwards.

Ian: So Erin, you thought he was your friend? Why would you think that?

Walton: That's how he gets them (pitched voice and holding his hand). He makes them think he is their friend. He's very convincing. You should know that, Ian.

Ian: All too well. How can we beat him? Any weaknesses of his that you have seen.

Walton: You can't. He's too strong! His powers date back before my time. I've been living way over a hundred years, too.

Ian picks up Walton and holds him by his collar.

Ian: You better think before my fiery hands burn through your shirt, then to your shoulders, taking both arms off.

Walton: Ok! I don't know all his powers. But I do know that his initial powers are Dreams themselves.

Ian: What does that mean?

Walton: He calls it lucid dreaming. Where he controls his dream, and that's how he's able to travel, meet people and control their dreams. That's how he finds them, locates them, and I get them and bring them to him.

Alisha: Sicko!

Ian: So his original powers are Dreams, so he uses his powers or the powers he stole to the fullest through his dreams. He's more powerful while sleep than awake.

Walton: I was never sure. I just did my jo-

Alisha: If I hear you say that one more time! I swear.

Ian: Well, it's time to meet him face to face. Walton, you are coming with us. Girls, let's go and stand behind me. You can tell me more as we get to the facility. We can make a plan against him on our way.

Ian grabs Walton by the collar and begins dragging him towards the mall entrance. As Ian walks underneath each skylight, his body turns into a fiery glow. Ian can feel the crowd of people looking at him. He can hear the whispers, and he can feel fear's presence among those. He can see the embarrassment on Erin's and Alisha's faces.

Walton begins to plea with Ian.

Walton: Just kill me! I failed him. He wants the girls, and I told you I couldn't care less about them. Just doing my job. I'm good as dead right now.

Ian: You should have thought about that a long time ago. It's not just about my girls. It's the others that you've harmed, too. I will ask this, are there anymore "partners" out there? People that might come after us or work with both of you?

Walton: Yes! But the strong ones, you want to avoid seeing them. They are just like you and him. Please just get it over with.

Ian: It will be all over soon.

Walton: No, you don't understand. If you walk out those doors with these girls, you might not-

Ian: Shut up! Not another word.

They finally reach the entrance. As they step out of the mall, they see more of Walton's Crew. They also see Nicole.

Alisha: Mom!

Erin: Mommy!

Ian freezes up. He sees "him." He's looking at the Dream Man.

Walton: I told you!

Silent for a second, then Nicole looks up.

Nicole: Oh My God! Alisha, Erin. (crying) Ian! You're glowing. I'm so sorry I should have-

Ian: Nicole. It's ok. We will get out of this.

Alisha: Is that him? In the black coat?

Ian: I can't tell; they all have on black coats. They all look the same too.

Alisha: Do you see the right one, Erin?

Erin: No. They look the same.

Ian: Get out of our way! I would rather not have to hurt any of you! You are all working for an evil, wicked man who preys on children and the weak and has done this for a very long time! Move!

Dream Man: (Talking through a henchman) Ian. You have put up one hell of a fight these last sixteen hours. You have shown these girls what resilience and endurance look like. For that, I must give you a hand, a round of applause, if I might. You defeated Walton twice and beat his men. Unfortunately, that is all that's rewarded for your efforts. You taught these girls a vital lesson: sometimes your will isn't always enough. Sometimes the end of the road is the end of the road. No, happily ever after, No continuation. Just the end. Don't look at it as a trial, but failure. Giving it your all doesn't result in success. This is your conclusion, my friend, Little Ian.

CHAPTER 10

Our Friend, Time

Hours ago, back at Nicole and Brian's house.

Nicole: Okay, so they are going to a pizza diner in Iowa. Sorry Brian, running behind, worried about the girls.

Brian: It's cool; let's just get going. I got our bags in the car; we can also stop by the police station on our way to your parents.

Brian: Who is it?

Silence.

Brian: Yes, who is it?

Nicole: Hey, whoever's out there, we have a gun. And we will shoot you if you don't stop trespassing.

Nicole goes to grab the shotgun. She is surprised when she's met with a henchman.

Nicole: Get out of my house! Now!

Henchman: Can't. He's here to see you.

Nicole: Brian!

At the front door, Brian hears another knock.

Nicole: Who is "He"!?

Henchman: (Smiling) Him!

The door unlocks from the outside. The Dream Man walks in, punches Brian, and sends him flying across the room.

Nicole: Brian!

Dream Man: Settle down! (Puts a knife towards Nicole's face) Just here to talk. Call them!

Nicole: Call who?

Dream Man looks at the henchman to grab Brian. He then stabs Brian in the arm.

Dream Man: Want to play games? I don't have time for games.

Brian: (yelling in pain) We know what you want! But you won't get them; they're long gone! And they know how to avoid you in dreams!

Dream Man: I'm impressed. You have figured my workout. (Looks at a henchman. The henchman then takes the knife and cuts Brian's other arm.)

Nicole: (Holding her face in her hands, crying.) STOP IT! You already know we won't talk. We've already beaten you at your own game. Now what? You kill us and lose your only leverage. You have no idea where they are headed!

Dream Man: You are right. I don't, but you will tell me, Nicole. Brian can only take so much pain.

Brian: Don't give them anything Nicole! I can handle whatever they have coming!

Dream Man: That tongue of yours will be the next to go if I hear another work from you, Mr. Bost.

Nicole: Someone will have to hear something. We have neighbors.

Dream Man: I've lived for centuries. This isn't my first rodeo, Nicole. I've mastered this. Manipulation is my specialty? No need, though. I'm old school, so this is what will happen.

Dream Man pulls a blade out and stabs Brian in the shoulder.

Brian: Ahhh!!!!!

Dream Man: So, where are they headed? I have a thousand more in this coat, so let's play, Nicole!

Nicole looks away as she hears Brian yelling.

Dream Man: Hard to watch, huh? The man you love is suffering. Until death do us part!

Brian: Ahh!

Nicole covers her ears.

Dream Man: No! You will hear every bit of pain from this man!

Brian: Ahh!

Dream Man: I think a tear is rolling down, Nicole. Have you ever seen your husband cry? This is the second man you have failed! You failed as a mother!

Brian: Ahh!

Dream Man: You've failed as a wife!

Brian: Ugh! Ugh!

Dream Man: I'm sure your parents are even disappointed in the woman you've become.

Nicole watches Brian suffer. She finally caves in.

Nicole: Minnesota… Plymouth, Minnesota. They're meeting with Brian's brother, Will…

Dream Man: Minnesota. You don't say, nice facility out there.

Nicole: Brian? I am so sorry!

Brian: I'll live.

Dream Man: Hey Brian, I just want to let you know, this could've all been avoided.

Brian: You sick son of

Dream Man: Hey now, no need for that. I just wanted to let you know. I'll send my condolences to Erin and Will.

Brian: What? How do you?

Dream Man: I said this could've been all avoided, I know everything. I just wanted to have a little fun with you and Nicole. See how long it will take her to break. So, thank you, Nicole. We'll clean this mess up. But first…

The Dream Man stabs Brian right in the chest.

Nicole: BRIAN!

Nicole runs after the Dream Man, but the henchman grabs her.

Dream Man: Take her with you, and drive until I give you a location. And you, Mrs. Nicole, time to sleep!

Present Time

Henchman: (Dream Man talking through him) Been a longtime Ian. These are my replicas. I can duplicate or multiply or, in other words…

Ian: (Frustrated) I get your ability! Seems like you are too scared to come face-to-face.

(Dream Man steps out of the henchman.)

Dream Man: Not ability, abilities! Keep that in mind. I can't fear either, remember that? You must still be in a rush. Very little to say.

Ian: Nothing to talk about. Let Nicole and us go, and I'll spare Walton's life. This is your only option. I don't think you want to deal with me like this, at this very sunny moment.

Dream Man: Not too concerned. Walton got his job done; he brought these girls to me. Not his ideal circumstances, but nonetheless, they're in my presence. I'll take them off your hands, head back to the DOP facility and start the process.

Ian: You have to now use modern technology to steal others' powers. So sad.

Dream Man: Well, for something like this, I've been preparing for, not even I'm going to stay stable for what I need to get those time traveling powers. So "my" company, DOP, has been researching for a long time for cases like this.

Ian: Your company, huh?

Dream Man: Yeah, DOP stands for Dream Of Powers. Such a small world. How their uncle is my employee. Things always come full circle, Ian. Let me ask you, girls, you too, Nicole, what does your Ian do for a living? Better question, who is Ian? Like, really, who is he? Husband, father, friend? How about a liar? How about broken? What about fearful?

Alisha: My Dad isn't afraid of anything and isn't any of those things either.

Dream Man: Alisha, nice to finally meet you. Thanks to you, I found out how strong Erin really was. And hi, little Erin. Been a few weeks. I'm still your friend even though you abandoned me, just like Big I did when he was young like you once.

Ian: You were very manipulative and went after me because you felt I was weak! That is why you go after any of your victims. You spot a weakness or sense that weakness.

Dream Man: I go for these powers because people are ungrateful for them! I don't care if you are young or old! Black or white! Power is power! That's what I want, and that's what I need. Unfortunately, the weaker ones are the ones that I felt sorry for. No one cared about you, Ian, after your parents died.

Ian: Actually, people did; you killed them too!

Dream Man: Aw yeah. I did, didn't I? Well, you seem to do good for yourself. And these girls that you're protecting, I get it. But they won't use their powers for any good or for any reason. I'm sure they don't even want them.

Ian: Well, they aren't weak; Walton can attest to that. They won't waste their powers. And they seem to appreciate them too. They just want to be careful with them.

Dream Man: Well, from what that little one tells me, Alisha isn't too fond of having powers. And Erin hasn't been too careful with her either. See, with Erin's powers, I can right all my wrongs or at least alter some of my decisions. Some of these powers aren't worth having. Like, I don't need to cook five-star meals every night. Planting money trees… None of that matters to me anymore. All that matters is more power.

Ian: And Alisha?

Dream Man: I can always know someone's next move. I'll know what to do, when, and even why I'm doing it. Their powers go hand in hand. To look beyond and control the past, present, and future. Then add your powers after all these years. I can go to places not even imaginable, other worlds! Endless possibilities with the Sun's powers. Hell, Ian, you don't even know how to use half of your gifts. So just hand them all over, and I'll be as gracious as possible with your deaths.

Erin looking for Brian.

Erin: Mommy! Where's daddy?

Dream Man: Aww, you don't know, do you, Erin? Had Big I stayed in contact with your mother and daddy; he might've been able to tell you. That goes back to who Big I really is. And what's he become.

Ian: Don't do this, don't tell her! (Lifts Walton up) if you say another word. I swear, his life will be over with.

Dream Man: Walton?

Walton: Yes, boss!

Dream Man: You have been one of the best. But he believes you are leverage. And what do we do with people who turn into leverage!

Walton: No! Please no! I've done everything you've asked; I've never failed. My crew has never failed you.

Dream Man: Sorry, Walton.

Dream Man releases his shadow, which grabs Walton and begins to take his powers. Walton's body stretches in and out and then turns into liquid. Ian watches while Nicole, Erin, and Alisha turn their heads. Erin covers her ears and starts to cry, hearing Walton scream out for help.

Dream Man: You have become numb from pain and desensitized to a crying voice over the years, Ian.

Ian: I have no sympathy for monsters. I intended to end him myself, for going after my kids. You'll be crying for mercy here, too.

Dream Man: Really?

Ian: Yeah. You finally see my power in its true form. The power that you never got to have. I've been waiting a long time to see you again.

Dream Man: Ha! I have more power than you could imagine. I'll get your powers finally, along with those girls too.

Erin: You won't be getting mine. Ian will beat you!

Dream Man: Aww. Little Erin, you are not my friend either anymore. I thought we were really becoming best friends. Mommy, did you know that? Erin is the reason I found you guys, too. Erin and I have been friends for the last few months. She tried to tell you all, but you all wouldn't believe her.

Nicole: Erin. Baby, I'm sorry. I should've listened to you.

Dream Man: Yeah! Kids usually are the most honest, but you ignore her. Alisha even didn't believe her. Speaking of which, (turning to Alisha) Hi little "Sunshine."

Alisha: Don't call me that!

Dream Man: Why? That's only what Daddy can call you? His parents used to call him that, too. Oh, it was "Dreamy." Before I killed them, Ian and I were friends too. I never got to be your friend, though, Alisha. Your mom, Brian, and I became close friends a few hours ago. But mommy didn't want to play fair. So I had to hurt Brian. Do we all see the connections here? Ian. It all came back full circle for you and me. It always goes full circle.

Erin: What happened to Daddy?

Dream Man: Sorry, little one. Daddy isn't here with us anymore.

Alisha: What?

Erin: What does that mean?

Dream Mam: It means daddy is gone; you won't see him anymore. Thanks to your mom and Ian.

Erin getting teary-eyed.

Alisha: (turning to Erin) Hey, it's going to be okay. Just stay calm, Erin. We can try to fix it later when we get back home.

Dream Man: Lies! More Lies! All you guys do is lie to one another. Try to comfort one another with lies.

Ian: That's enough talking! You've said enough!

Ian charges toward Dream Man. Dream Man counters by having some of his duplicates turning into brick pillars. Ian breaks through the pillars and kicks Dream Man with a flying kick.

Alisha: Yes! He got him, Erin! (Alisha turns to Erin and sees Erin's facial expression is very displeased.) It's going to be okay, Erin.

Erin stays silent.

Dream Man: (picking himself off the ground) Ugh. Okay. That was okay. (Turns to Nicole) Was that satisfying?

Nicole: Yep!

Ian: I don't remember you talking this much!

Dream Man: Try that again and watch what happens.

Ian: With Pleasure!

Ian goes for another flying kick.

Dream Man: Gotcha!

Dream Man opens up a shadow portal. Ian flies right in.

Alisha: Daddy!

Nicole: Where did you take him? Where did he go?

Dream Man: Where he belongs until I get done with these two. He will be going through a Dream loop of his sufferings and failures. Just to remind him that I've won.

Dream Man begins walking toward Alisha and Erin.

Alisha: (Turns to Erin) Erin.

Erin: (sniffling and wiping her tears) Yeah?

Alisha: Can you open that portal back up?

Erin: Can I what?

Alisha: Reverse time again, too open that portal to grab dad out. We need him. We don't have much time.

Erin: I can't, Alisha. That's what I was telling you earlier. I don't know why, but I can't do it again.

Alisha: Please! You have to try, Erin! It's our only way to get dad back and beat this monster. If he takes us to that place. We won't ever go back home and try to save your Dad.

Alisha quickly thinks of a plan.

Alisha: It's okay, Erin. You are too scared, probably just like your dad was before he died.

Erin: What?

Dream Man: That was cold "Sunshine," even for someone like me.

Nicole: Alisha, why would you say that?

Erin: That was mean to say, Alisha.

Alisha: So!

Erin: So don't be mean!

Alisha: My dad is gone, all because your Dad couldn't protect us and was too afraid to take us himself. Just like you're too scared to help us now.

Erin: Stop being MEAN!

Erin screams. As she screams, everything around her moves slowly. Dream man was just about to reach them, but is stopped.

Dream Man: Whaaaaatttt. Iiiiiissss. Ttthhhhhhiiiiiisssss.

Alisha hears and sees the Dream Man moving slowly. She realizes that they bought some time.

Alisha: Okay, Erin, it's just you and me. Everyone else is moving slower. I take back all those things I said earlier. I'm sorry, I was just trying to upset you, so you can do your hand thing and bring my dad back.

Erin: So you were just being a meanie?

Alisha: Yes, just teasing you like always. I took it a little too far, but it was the only way to do this. I didn't think this would happen, but now we can focus on opening that Dream portal again.

Alisha takes Erin's hand and starts walking toward Nicole. Passing by Dream Man as well.

Alisha: Okay, Erin. Let's open it back up. I believe you can do this. Just rewind time again, like you did inside the mall. Let's try to do this as quickly as possible; I don't know how long you can do this. And Dream man is about to be turning back towards us.

Dream Man: Stoooppp. Ttttheeemmm!!!

Some Dream man duplicates begin to close in on Alisha and Erin.

Nicole: Giiiiirrrllss!

Alisha: Let's do this, sis.

Erin: I don't know if I can do that again.

Alisha: Let me help you. Lift both arms up.

Erin lifts both arms up.

Alisha: Now, open your hands.

Erin opens her hands.

Alisha: Now push! Push the air as hard as you can.

Erin: Okay. Like this?

Erin pushes, but just as the henchman begins to move closer. As Erin pushes the air hard, she starts a shock wave that hits the Dream man duplicates, instantly turning them old and then into dust.

Erin: Woah!

Alisha: Wow! Okay, wrong way. This time, hold, push the air but pull back as quick as you can.

Erin: How do you know this will work?

Alisha: I love physics! Honestly, I think it would be cool. Come on, let's see it.

Erin raises her arms again, holds out her hands, and pushes that air, but quickly pulls back and rips the air to open a small portal.

Alisha: Yes! Now, open it up some more!

Erin (struggling) I can't! This is too much for me. It hurts just holding this!

Alisha grabs Erin by the waist and begins to pull her back. As she's pulling her back, the Dream Man's portal gets wider.

Alisha: C'mon, Erin! Hold on! We are almost there! We almost got it open!

Erin begins to have tears roll down her face. She begins to sweat and get very hot. She and Alisha both fall back. Erin lands on Alisha, and Alisha feels Erin's scorching hands on her arm.

Alisha: Owww! Get off! Get off! Get off! Erin, please get up!

Erin: Okay! Okay! Sorry.

Alisha and Erin stand up and look at the dark purple portal.

Alisha: WOW! You did this, Erin. This is so cool!

Nicole: Girls! Lookout!

Dream Man grabs Alisha's and Erin's heads.

Dream Man: Yeah. I'm going to need that power.

Just as Dream Man's about to teleport them, Nicole comes charging at Dream Man with a tackle, taking him down to the ground.

Nicole: (jumping up from the ground) Let's go, girls! Let's get Ian back!

As Nicole and the girls stand in front of the portal. They hesitate for a second.

Nicole: Maybe this isn't such a good idea. Ian could be dead now.

Alisha: No turning back now, Mom. We have to try.

They all hold hands. Nicole steps in first, then Erin walks in. But before Alisha can step in, Dream Man grabs her and pulls her hair.

Dream Man: I'm not losing! You're coming with me!

Erin: Alisha!

CHAPTER 11

Ian's Nightmares

As Nicole and Erin float through the Dream portal, they watch the memories in their lives. They notice the dreams they've had, the nightmares they've encountered, and the fantasies that will never happen, but what they think of all the time.

Nicole's fantasies of what life would have been like had she pursued her love for dancing. She sees herself dancing and performing in front of millions of people, receiving flowers and getting a standing ovation. She has a tear rolling down her face.

Erin: You were a dancer, mommy?

Nicole: I wanted to be. I loved dancing. I danced at church, had recitals, and wanted to study it in college. I was practicing my first solo ever, and I just knew I would nail it, and this was finally going to be my time to shine; I might get an offer from a school or something since my grades were great too. Well, during one of my rehearsals, one of my instructors was just so hard on me. So finally, she pulled me to the side and asked me if I couldn't hit every move with perfection or if I was by a tenth of a second. I would be cut, not lose my solo, but get cut. So, I practiced 24/7. All the time, during school lunch. I went to bed very late every night practicing. I really wanted to get this done and felt like I had the opportunity to do so. I even missed church for this, and that was the problem. Once I started missing church, my parents pulled me out and told me I was letting dance take over my life when dancing was my life. I even showed the hard instructor, and she saw I had got it down to perfection, she tried to convince my parents, but they said it was taking over my life when the "church" should be my focus.

Erin: So you never danced again?

Nicole: No, I focused on church and school only from then on. That was the only importance in my life. So I accepted that. I smiled and laughed and kept on going with life. But I wasn't happy, and sometimes it makes me sad that I never got to live that out. Now I love you girls and couldn't imagine the world without you both. I'm going to have to get used to your dad not being around now, too. But mommy had dreams of her own, and they were taken away too.

Erin: Sorry, mommy.

Nicole: It's okay, sweetie. I truly have accepted this, but I wonder how different life could've been for all of us. I never told anyone this, not even your father. So remember, Erin, shoot for your dreams and live them out. I will never try to block them.

Erin nods her head.

Erin: Okay, mommy.

They finally reach Ian. They stop on a rocky road that then turns into a clear pathway. They see the sky, but they notice it's a very dark, cloudy sky. They begin to levitate and float in the dark sky. They hear Ian's voice.

Ian: C'mon, Ian! C'mon! Uhhhh!!!! They need you; they need you more than ever now! You got this; you got this, don't give up! You can't give up! Uhhhhh!!!! They're depending on you! You have to save the day; you need to save the day! You made it this far! She needs you more than ever now!!

Nicole: Ian! What is that on you!

Ian: How? How did you find me? The portal closed behind me!

Nicole: Erin opened the portal back up. But Alisha was taken just as we got in! We need to get you out of here-

As Nicole and Erin locate Ian, they see a boulder on Ian's back. Ian also has his hands and ankles chained down. The heavy boulder could crush Ian if his arms or legs give out. He also can't stand up because of the chains.

Nicole: Oh my goodness, Ian, what can we do to help?

Ian: I don't know. I'm trying to figure out a way. I'm trying not to quit or give up. There seems to be no other option, though.

Nicole: Don't talk like that! We will get you out. You have to get out! He's got Alisha!

Ian: Where's Erin?

Erin: I'm here.

Ian: Did you both see things while getting here?

Nicole: Yes.

Erin: Yes.

Ian: Dreams? Nightmares? What could've been?

Nicole: Yes, Ian, what does that have to do with anything? We need to get you out of here!

Ian: That's the thing, Nicole; look down towards your ankles, wrist, or any part of your body. Just look.

Nicole and Erin both examine their bodies.

Nicole: I have nothing around me!

Erin: Mommy! There is a chain around my waist. I can't go anywhere now! I can't move!

Erin begins to panic.

Nicole: Oh my! Okay, baby, hold on, just hold on! Ian! What is happening? Why does she have that around her?

Ian: Keep her calm; I panicked earlier. That's how I got all this around me, too. It could be because of the panic, or it could be much more than that.

Nicole: Like what?

Ian: Bondage! We must be holding something in. A long time ago, that star that I received from the sun. Told me to always tell the truth and live out my truth. Be honest with even ourselves, we can fool everyone, but we can never fool ourselves!

Nicole: Live out your truth? Be honest, what does all this mean?

Ian: I am powerful, Nicole. Sometimes I believe I can use my powers without the sunlight shining on me. I just haven't figured it out yet. I'm scared to figure it out. I'm scared of numerous things. I think Dream

Man sent me here to stay captive. He knows me better than what I said before. He knows that I think of my parents daily. He knows that sending me here, like I'm sure others who tried to fight back would be stuck here because they are afraid of the truth. They're afraid to tell the truth about themselves or anything that scares them.

Erin: Mommy! I'm scared! I really am scared!

Nicole: I know, my love, we will get you out! Ian, tell me what we need to do!

Ian: We need to tell the truth. What's holding us back are our lies. I saw visions of my parents. What could've been growing up with them in my life. I try to forget about them, but I miss them. I miss them so very much. I miss being a boy and not having a care in the world. I missed everything before my world fell apart. I thought you helped put it back together, but I still wanted my mom and dad back. That's what I wanted. I wanted a childhood with no suffering or pain or loss. I was robbed of that. And since I never addressed this, it's led to adulthood that I sometimes feel I'm failing miserably at.

Nicole: Ian. It's ok to feel this way; I neve-

Ian: Let me finish, Nicole. I need to say these things. Just hold on to Erin. Comfort her. I'm not telling you this or her for your good, but because I've been lying to myself all these years.

Nicole goes to comfort and calm Erin down. Erin is crying hysterically.

Ian: Okay, here we go. Erin, I have blamed you before for our breakup. Embarrassing enough, I still blame you, but what I said before was true too. I think you are a brave and wonderful kid. And I'm sorry for making you feel so bad; your intuition was right. My insecurities and fear have led us here. With Alisha imprisoned, we imprisoned, and many innocent lives lost, including Brian's. For that, Little E and Nicole, I'm truly sorry.

Nicole: We forgive you, don't we, Erin?

Erin: Ye... Yes, I forgive you, Big I!

Ian's left ankle is released from the chain. Ian doesn't notice, though.

Ian: I've struggled with acceptance and being loved. Nicole, what happened wasn't right, of course, but I was never there for you. It was one thing, just being us two. But when Alisha came, I avoided being the father she needed and the husband you prayed for. I don't know my daughter as well. I love Alisha, and if she dies for a second time today, it will be all because of my mistakes. I always wondered if I was being a good example, showing enough love, or spending enough time with her. This journey showed I haven't, and some self-reflection is what I've been seeing since being chained up in my own mind or dream or wherever he's left us at. That was very hard for me to admit, but it's true.

Ian's right ankle is now released. Nicole gets teary-eyed.

Ian: My childhood felt like a failure. My marriage failed. And I'm failing as a father. Nicole, this is what I don't share because I'm afraid to let anyone down. Frightened that regardless of what I do or who I help or even love, I will fail at the end. Afraid It will lead to disappointment.

Ian's right wrist is released.

Ian: I know I said this, but I don't know how to defeat him. I'm the reason my parents and foster parents are dead. I could've prevented them from being killed. But I was too scared to do anything about it. I could've given up my powers, and they would still be here. When I finally knew his true motives, he offered me their lives for my powers. And I gave them up for that. That's the truth, Nicole. I sacrificed my childhood for these powers. And I still haven't done right with them.

Nicole: No! No! No! Ian, your parents were going to be gone regardless. He killed Brian, even after I gave you three up. You were also a child; you did what any child might've done.

Ian's left hand is released.

Ian: I'm not so sure. I'm showing more fear than I ever have now that Alisha is out there with him alone.

Nicole: We all are afraid of something, Ian. I was afraid to approach you that day in the lunchroom. We all heard stories about you, and I was afraid of what our peers would think of me if I hung out with you. But I did it anyway because I saw nothing but good in you. I saw the hurt and anger, of course. But I also saw a young man trying to get the piece of his life back together. Life hasn't been fair to you, Ian. However I have never met anyone with so much resilience. You can beat him, but not once did we say you have to do it alone.

Erin: Mommy, Ian! He told me that too, Ian. He told me that he would hurt everyone if I didn't give up my powers. We would go to places in my dreams, and I thought he was my friend. But friends would never hurt you, right? That's what Alisha told me.

Ian: Is that how Alisha has seen you two? Is that when Alisha told mommy and Brian?

Erin: (crying) Yes! I thought he was really my friend. I liked having powers and going back in time. He showed me everything, your life, Ian and Mommies.

Nicole: Wait, what?

Erin: I'm sorry, mommy, I knew you were a dancer and loved to dance; he showed me.

Ian: You danced?

Nicole: Long time ago. Let's stay focused.

Erin: Ian, I've seen you hurt people at your job. He made me watch too.

Ian: Watch what? He made you watch what, Erin?

Erin: You and your parents. I'm sorry I didn't say anything! (crying)

Ian: It's okay to cry, Erin! Cry! Do what I couldn't do. I thought crying was for the weak, but I now know that the strongest ones can show emotions. You are much stronger than I was, Erin. Look at your waist.

Erin's chains have been released.

Ian: You told the truth. Good job, little E!

Nicole: Ian, if you think you had so much weight on your shoulders, you forgot what it feels like not to hold a burden. Take a look at your hands. Nothing's there! You finally told yourself the truth, and now it's time to bring the truth to him. Stand up!

Ian finally rises.

Ian: My back! God, that was a lot weighing me down. Let's get out of here and come up with a plan! Little E, can you get us out of here?

Erin: I think so!

Ian: Good! I need to call someone when we get out of here! It's time to end this with him!

Dream Man and Alisha teleport inside the facility.

Alisha: All this trouble just to see the future or change your past?

Dream Man: Not any trouble for me. This just opened up endless possibilities for me.

Alisha: What possibilities? Giving back those powers and lives you've stolen in the past? Sparing those kids who never had a fighting chance! The thing I don't understand is why don't you go for adults? Or people in power who are doing more harm to the world, like you? Why kids?

Dream Man: I do! It doesn't matter if you're a child or the oldest dreamer in the world. Children are naïve and easily manipulated, yes! But adults aren't hard to target, either. Find the right one who doesn't realize their potential or hasn't discovered their powers yet. That's who I target.

Alisha: So why didn't you ever target me? I don't want these powers, never asked for this.

Dream Man: I know you didn't. So ungrateful for what you have, ignoring others that are going without. This is why I say we aren't so different. You judge me, though? HA!

Alisha: That's totally different!

Dream Man: I've heard that before, too, from your Dad. And we all know that's not true. But what is true is that I didn't need to target you. You haven't been as nice to your sister, and I see that. I noticed her being a loner, just like your dad. I saw her unable to make friends, just like your dad! You think you were protecting her from me when you were really pushing her towards a new friend! So thank you, Alisha! Feel bad; you should; this is your fault too, little Sunshine.

CHAPTER 12

Time Matters

Dream Man looks at the employees in the facility!

Dream Man: Listen up! I know we started off wrong today with some of your colleagues being killed! That were those who wanted to question me, my powers, and my position in this company! You all work for ME! I've invested a lot for this day to come, finally! You all have been paid very lucrative and worked hard to research how to transfer powers from one person to another.

Alisha: Why would they need to? You've been taking powers all this time!

Dream Man: (Turning to Alisha) I'm getting to that, Alisha! I'm very much older than you can imagine. With that being said, I'm not sure how much more time I have left. I have plans and things that I need to change in the past. Only one true thing matters to me, and that's time.

Alisha: You'll get her powers over my dead body!

Dream Man: That's the plan! This also is why you are a bonus! Once I get your powers, I'll be able to see things, all things. Enemies, natural disasters! Hell, even disgruntled employees that want to rebel against me. I'll be able to see that and do something about it before it even happens. (Turns back to the employees) So I hope everyone is ready! I hope everything is prepared! This is the beginning of a new age for me! I'm going to take her powers; you all will see her die!

Dream Man begins to duplicate himself.

Dream Man: If any of you tries anything besides your jobs, I will kill you too! Her first! Then the little one, when I get back! Then that man living with a star in him! Oh, can anyone tell me how long the process will take?

Employee: Well, none of us have been working in this department! You killed everyone that was working in the power transfer department, all but one, Will. But we don't know where Will is.

Dream Man: Oh! Well, I'll find him. Let's just get her to sleep!

Ian, Nicole, and Erin finally get out of the portal.

Ian: Wow, Erin, that is amazing. It truly is.

Erin: Thanks, Ian!

With daylight still out, the sun is still shining. Ian begins to feel somewhat strange.

Nicole: Are you okay, Ian?

Ian: Yeah, I just feel weird. It could've been that portal we were in.

Erin: Why aren't you glowing again? The sun is still out!

Ian: I'm not angry. Or feel angry. Whatever happened in that portal feels like it actually helped me.

Nicole: You're not angry? Even with Alisha being held hostage by that monster?

Ian: Not angry, but prompt. Ready to get our baby back and end this.

Nicole: Well, I'm pissed, ready to break his neck! So, we need to get there quickly; how far away are we from the facility?

Ian: Not too far.

Nicole: So, do we take a car? Or what? Can you jump very high? Or fly? What's the play here, Ian?

Ian: I can do those things, but not as quickly as we need to get there. But Erin can probably get us there a lot faster.

Erin: I can?

Erin: I can?

Ian: Yes, you can. Erin, you can rewind time. From the sounds of it, you can also freeze time, right? That's how you open Dream Man's portal to get me back. So, you did that, not in a dream, by the way, in the real world.

Nicole: What are you saying?

Ian: I'm saying Erin can manipulate time like it's a hobby. Remember earlier, Erin, when I was explaining using our phones or electronics and how they could track us if we did.

Erin: Yes.

Ian: Okay, so use your powers to pinpoint where Alisha is. Like a phone can GPS us to a place. Gps us to Alisha. Does that make any sense?

Erin: Huh?

Nicole: Yeah, Ian, I'm even confused. We don't even know where the Facility is at now.

Ian: You're right. Okay, how about this. Close your eyes, Erin.

Erin closes her eyes

Erin: Closed.

Ian: Now, think of Alisha.

Erin: Thinking.

Ian: So, think of Alisha and think of what she was wearing and what she smelled like, and what she looked like before she was taken away by him.

Erin is now imagining Alisha. She heard Alisha scream right before she was taken.

Ian: Do you see her?

Erin: I see her! I can hear her too! I hear the scream she did before he took her away.

Ian: Great! Now, follow her.

Erin, with her eyes still closed, begins to walk the trail that Dream Man dragged Alisha away. She watches it all.

Erin: He has her by her hair. She's yelling for help. She tries to fight back, but she can't. (A tear rolls down her face.)

Ian wipes the tear away for Erin.

Ian: What happens next?

Erin: They stop right here. He grabs her head, and they fall to the ground, but then they are gone. What happened to them?

Ian: They teleported. Keep your eyes closed and stay focused, little E. Rewind a little bit, and see Alisha again.

Erin: Okay.

Ian: Do you see her again? Does Dream man have her before they hit the ground?

Erin: Yes.

Ian: Good, now take your hands. Push where Alisha is standing, then pull really hard. I mean, as hard as you can!

Erin: Like Alisha had me do before? Like how we found you?

Ian smiling.

Ian: Exactly like that. The only difference is that you aren't angry or sad this time. You're focused. Now pull.

Erin pushes then, pulls where Alisha's standing, and rips open a portal to the facility.

Nicole: Oh my goodness. That was amazing, Erin! You did it!

Erin: I did! I did it again!

Ian: Great job, Erin! Now, tell your mom it's time to go to sleep.

Nicole: What?

Erin touches Nicole's arm and instantly puts her to sleep.

Erin: Sorry, mommy.

Ian: She'll be okay; we don't want her to get hurt. Mr. Zip will come to pick her up from here. He's on his way. Do you remember the plan? You must sleep and keep him busy. And I will be here in the real world. Okay?

Erin: Yes, sir.

Ian takes his tracker and places it next to Nicole.

Ian: He'll be able to find her here.

Erin: How will he find us?

Ian: I have a signal for that. Trust me, he'll find us. Let's go.

Ian and Erin step into the portal and step out onto the DOP facility's ground. The portal closes behind them.

Ian pulls his building scan device out. Throws the device out towards the facility. The device shows nothing except for a helicopter on the top of the building.

Ian: Damn.

Erin: What's wrong?

Ian: My device won't show us where they are or what it did before at the diner. This facility must be heavily guarded. Hopefully, Mr. Zip won't have a hard time finding us here.

Erin: What now?

Ian: We go straight through the front door!

Erin: The sun is bright right now.

Ian: Right before it sets. This is going to get ugly, but we got this!

Erin: I know.

Ian: Good, let's do this!

Ian and Erin begin to walk toward the front entrance.

Ian: Hey! Hey! Hey coward! Still asleep?

Dream Man duplicate opens the door.

Dream Man: Of course I am; I can wake up if you need me to, though.

Ian: I'll find you and wake you up myself!

Dream Man: You are relentless! Erin is too. Man, that power will do wonders for me.

Alisha: Dad, we're on the third floo--

Dream Man: Oh, be quiet! I was going to tell him. She spoiled it, but yes, we're on the third floor, you know. One below the top floor, two above the first one.

Ian: I can count. Why don't you wake up, and we can have a good ol' one-on-one?

Dream Man: Oh, we're going to have that! I'm going to finally get your powers, too!

Ian: Maybe you are just overrated!

Dream Man: Cut the crap. Get up here, so I can kill you, the scientist, the doctors, and all these other hypocrites who pretend to help and care but ultimately bow down to the almighty dollar.

Ian: They are in the presence of the world's greatest hypocrite, then. You might not care for money, but you've been the biggest waste this world has ever seen. Your potential and powers are all in vain!

Dream Man: This will be for nothing. All the suffering and pain I've brought won't be for nothing.

Ian: Give me my child back! This is the last time I will say it!

Dream Man: Little Ian! This will bring me joy, killing you!

Ian runs towards the front entrance and tackles the duplicate to the ground. Erin sneaks behind Ian, then runs towards the west wing, and searches for a place to hide. As Erin is running, she hears a familiar voice call her name quietly.

Familiar voice: Erin! Erin! It's uncle, Will.

Erin: Uncle William? Are you tricking me? Is this the dream, Man?

Will: No! It's really me. Why are you running around here alone? It's not safe with these bad people here. Where are Ian and Alisha?

Erin: Ian's out there fighting some bad guys. And Alisha's been here. The Dream Man took her. Ian and I just got here. I opened a portal and got us here.

Will: A portal? You opened a portal? Amazing! Look, it's still not safe, you should stay with me. And stay quiet before someone hears us. They are everywhere!

Erin: Ian was going to be fighting Dream Man. He said he would try to find you and Alisha. I was going to sleep.

Will: Sleep? This isn't a time to sleep, niece.

Erin: You don't understand. That's part of the plan. Ian calls it some type of dream where I can control things in them.

Will: Lucid Dreaming!

Erin: Yeah! Well, he said that I could go into the Dream Man's dream too while he's asleep and start going back into his past and taking his powers away.

Will: How would you do that?

Erin: I will just freeze time again. Ian said right before Dream Man takes power, he freezes time and takes them. It's a lot easier to freeze time in my dreams, and it's fun too.

Will: I get it. So he's going to be occupied fighting, chasing, and attempting to kill Ian. Still trying to find you and me. And keep Alisha hostage. That's a lot on his plate, even with those duplicates.

Erin: Why is he looking for you, Uncle William?

Will: Because I'm the one that knows how to control the machines to transfer your powers from your bodies to his. This entire time I've been working for a monster; I had no idea, though, Erin.

Erin: It's okay, Uncle William. You won't have to work for him anymore. We will beat him.

Will: I believe we can, too. Now when you get to him and take his powers, they will look like a ball of light, maybe different colors of some sort. You will be able to tell that it holds some type of power.

Erin: Okay. Will it be heavy, or will it hurt?

Will: I'm not sure. It might feel heavy or strange, or might feel like nothing. I've never touched energy like that with my bare hands. I've always transferred them using tools and machines.

Erin: How should I hold it then and carry all of his powers?

Will: Well, since you will be in your dream and can control them. Think of something that you can hold onto them with.

Erin: My baggie. Can I use my baggie?

Will: You can use just about whatever you think will work. Just be careful.

Erin: Yes, sir.

Will: Oh, one other thing. Do not help or save anyone in his past. They are already gone, or something far worse is happening to them. Just take the powers, and go.

Erin: Okay. Do you think Alisha is sleeping now?

Will: I highly doubt it. Why do you ask?

Erin: Ian wants her to sleep; that's part of the plan too. She was awake when Ian tackled that bad guy. I heard her talking.

Will: So y'all need her sleep?

Erin: Yep.

Will: Okay. It's risky, but I trust your plan. So, I guess I need to get caught to do my part.

Erin: Okay! Hey Uncle William. Before you go, can you do something for me?

Will: Yes, Erin?

Erin: Can you keep talking to help me go to sleep. You are kind of boring to talk to, Uncle William.

Will: Umm. Sure. Wait. Is that a good or ba-

Erin: Thank you. Tell me a quick story, please. (Erin lays down)

Will: You're welcome, I guess.

Ian continues to fight with Dream Man's duplicates. One duplicate runs in but gets put into a chokehold. Ian then picks the duplicate up by the neck in the chokehold and tosses him into the other duplicates.

Ian: Will the fight continue like this? Me fighting replicas of you? That's not even as strong as you!

Dream Man: You'll eventually tire out. One of my duplicates will find their Uncle. And I will get those powers.

Ian: What's the need for her uncle, then? Why didn't you take their powers long ago?

Alisha: He's afraid, Dad! He wants them to change his past; something's off with him. That's why!

Ian: Aww. I see the true motives. You have been power hungry, sure. But you are afraid? You aren't too certain what is your fate.

Dream Man scolding Ian.

Ian: What? No answer? Finally speechless?

Dream Man: (smirking) You do not know how much of an asset you would've been.

Ian: Like Walton was?

Dream Man: Better. I've had other allies. Strong ones too. Very gifted and grew to be as ruthless as me. But none of what you have become or would've been.

Ian: That won't work on me anymore. I'm not that child anymore that you manipulated.

Dream Man: Oh, I know you are a man. A father now. So, you have a lot to lose and nothing to gain.

Ian: And you do?

Dream Man: I have goals, too, despite what you think of me. I've fought evil and battled monsters. These powers will continue to battle those long after you all are gone. Wars I've been a part of, controlled, and ended; these are nothing compared to what might be coming.

Ian: Such as?

Dream Man: It doesn't matter. You won't be here to see what might or might not come!

Dream Man and Ian both charge at each other. Dream Man pulls some throwing knives out and flicks them at Ian. Ian dodges a few knives, then catches one to throw back at Dream Man.

Meanwhile, Erin finally falls asleep. Will sneaks out of the room undetected. Will begins to run down the hall.

Will: I need to get out of here! I need help!

Ian and Dream Man hear Will. Dream Man gives the nod to one of his duplicates to get Will.

Dream Man: Just the man I was looking for!

CHAPTER 13

Power of a Dream

Erin sits up in her dream. She sees Will being caught and dragged upstairs. Erin goes from room to search for Dream Man. She's having a hard time locating him, so she decides to search for him using her tracking powers.

Erin's POV: Okay, Erin, just try to feel where he is at. Just like Alisha. You can do this.

Erin then hears heartbeats. She hears people conscious's and thoughts. She hears the fear in some people's heads. The uncertainty that they will make it home. She can hear the cries and pain that some are in. She then feels and hears Ian's thoughts. She hears Ian's confidence growing as he continues to battle Dream Man. She then hears Dream Man's thoughts. She hears how he will plan to use his fire and shadow ability to beat Ian, since the knives and hand-to-hand combat won't work. She stays focused on Dream Man's thoughts, which lead to his heartbeat pattern. She hears his heart, racing and beating faster. And then she finally locates where the Dream Man's body is at.

Erin's POV: Second floor, last room in the Ea…Ea… East wing? The big room. That's what I'll call it.

Erin opens a portal to the room. She finally finds him, his physical body lying across the table. She gets her goodie bag out. She walks up to him and opens up a small portal to his memories.

Erin POV: Hmm. Where do I start? How do I start? How do I get to his beginning? Oh, wait, I got it.

Erin changes the way the portal looks to how images look on her tablet. She then swipes right to see his past.

Erin POV: Here we go. Just what I was looking for.

Erin continues to swipe right and is saddened by what she sees. She first goes back to see Brian's final moments. She sees how brave he was before he died. She proceeds to swipe right, but comes to a stop when she finally sees a little boy showing his powers to Dream Man.

Dream Man: Okay, now, Daren, are you ready to show me your powers now?

Daren: Yes. I guess.

Dream Man: Don't be afraid either; remember, this is just a dream, and I'm your friend, so don't be embarrassed.

Daren then drops to one knee, places the palms of both of his hands on the ground, closes his eyes to focus, and then crackling noises begin to be heard. The crackling noises become louder, and then a roaring blaze shoots Daren up onto his feet. His hands have a fire coming out of them.

Daren: (Joyful) I did it! Look, I did it! You see that!

Dream Man: (Calmly) Sure did. Impressive. You finally have them. Good for you.

Daren: So what's next?

Dream Man: You might not like what comes next.

Daren: Why not?

Dream Man begins to walk toward Daren.

Daren: Why not? Why are you looking like that? Did I do something wrong? Friend? Did I do something wrong?

Erin swipes right quickly before Dream Man approaches Daren.

Erin POV: Whew.

Erin continues to swipe right, and she sees some more children, just like Daren and just like her. Erin sees some crying and pleading for help. Pleading for their parents. She sees some trying to fight back with their powers, but are overmatched by Dream Man. Each time she watches, the sadness grows for them. She finally mustards up the courage to take one of his powers. She stops at the memory of him battling a young girl named Chloe. She has the ability to change the direction of the wind.

Chloe: I thought you were my friend. Why are you doing this?

Dream Man: I need them, Chloe. That's why!

Chloe keeps striking and knocking Dream Man off balance with the strong winds. She's keeping a distance between them. Dream Man finally knocks her off balance by shaking the ground underneath her.

Dream Man then builds four dirt pillars around Chloe. The pillars corner Chloe.

Chloe: What are you doing?

Dream Man: Improvising!

As Dream Man enters the dirt pillars with Chloe, she begins to cry. Erin can feel the fear coming from Chloe. Dream Man points at Chloe. She then becomes stiff and can no longer move of her own will.

Dream Man: This won't take long at all!

Chloe: Please don't do this!

The outline of Chloe's body goes dark purple. She screams as the outlining begins to form into a ball. A floating ball of energy emerges.

Erin's POV: That's it! That's what I need.

Erin freezes the Dream Man right before the ball of energy gets to him. Erin squeezes through the pillars and opens her goodie bag with both hands. And catches the energy power. She tightens up the bag and runs back through the portal. Closing it behind her.

Erin: OMG, I did it. I can't wait to tell them how I did this. They won't believe me. Onto the next.

While Erin has been on the Dream mission, Will finally reaches Alisha. One of Dream Man's duplicates grabbed him and tossed him to where Alisha was being held.

Will: Alright, man. I'm here.

Dream Man duplicate: Get to work! Or we start killing this department, too.

Alisha: Uncle Will? Do you know how to run this?

Will: Yeah. Didn't know I was working for a maniac, though! Sorry Alisha, but you should go to sleep. (Will winks at Alisha)

Alisha: What?

Will: Trust me, go to sleep, and it will be less painful.

Alisha: Where's Erin? And where is my Dad? Do they need help?

Will: (whispering) They got it figured out, and it's time for us to do our part. Just go to sleep. Trust me.

Alisha: Okay.

Ian and Dream Man continue their fight. Dream Man is using his throwing knives to stop Ian's momentum and keeping Ian at a distance. Ian is evading the knives, but can't get close.

Ian POV: What can I do to get closer? I'm going to eventually tire out. I am also going to need some sunlight too. It's pretty dark in here.

Dream Man: Thinking of that sunshine, huh?

Ian: I'm. Thin- Thinking of how much- Of. Of a coward, you are. I thought this was going to be hand to hand.

Dream Man: That's what you want, huh?

Dream Man tosses a knife to his left towards Ian. Ian stops in his tracks. Dream Man teleports to Ian's left and punches him in the ribs. Following up with a leg sweep, Ian hits the ground hard. Dream Man then kicks Ian across the floor.

Dream Man: Get up! C'mon get up!

Ian jumps to his feet

Ian: That's all you got?

Dream Man: (smirking) We can cut it out with the tough guy act. It's just you and me. You might've been able to give the girls hope, but you know how this will end.

Ian: I can imagine what might happen. But I must thank you. Whatever portal you placed me in showed me more about myself than I ever realized. It showed me the truth about myself. I might not be any better than you. I was shown all the people I've hurt, harmed, and killed. I was shown anger as a man that I never get to express. The anger that's bottled in. All because of you.

Dream Man: You're welcome then.

Ian: Yeah, I sometimes forget what I am or what I can be. I had a visitor come to see me when I was chained down.

Dream Man: Sure, Nicole and Erin saved you. I was planning to keep you there for a long time too.

Ian: Yeah, they did, but right before they got to me. This star that was given to me, that the Sun gifted in me, had a talk with me. The star asked, why haven't I used him yet? I honestly didn't understand what it was asking me. I use it, or at least I thought I did. I just thought that when the sun hits me, that's when the star shines brightest. That's when I get my glowing look.

Dream Man: Ha. You mean that look when you came out of that mall? Do you think I want your powers for that? No! I want those powers because you don't deserve them. The sun chose a fool! And that star. That star that's living in you won't help you! It won't tell you that. You don't have a clue of what your powers can do, and you don't just need the "sun" to fully show what you are capable of.

Ian: Oh, I'm aware of that now. (smiling)

Ian balls his right fist up, and his arm begins to glow fiery orange.

Ian: See, what you didn't want me to know, is that this star is a weapon that I have neglected to use. Just like those knives of yours, or sword of yours is stored somewhere in you. I have those things too.

Ian's right arm shoots out a fiery cutlass sword.

Dream man pulls his sword out.

Dream Man: This just got even more interesting.

Erin finally reaches Alisha in her dream.

Erin: Alisha. Alisha!

Alisha: OMG, Erin, you are okay. I thought the Dream Man had caught you.

Erin: No.

Alisha: How did you find me?

Erin: You are my sister; I always know where you are at!

Alisha smiles and hugs Erin.

Erin: But look what I found.

Alisha: What is it?

Erin: This is Dream man's powers!

Alisha: How? What? How did you get them? What are those powers?

Erin: Uhm, well, I took some water powers, and then some stuff that makes people do things. He had a lot of the same powers.

Alisha: Like super strength?

Erin: Yeah! Why would he need that?

Alisha: It doesn't matter; we have them now.

Erin: Do you want some?

Alisha: No! Keep those hidden away in your dreams somewhere. My Dad is fighting him now. Uncle Will told me to go to sleep, so you can give me some if I don't want any. Did you take any?

Erin: Uhm, maybe.

Alisha: What did you take?

Erin: I don't know. Something.

Alisha: Okay, just wake us up before they start the machines up.

Erin: Okay.

Ian and Dream Man continue their fight. Dream Man surrounds Ian with his duplicates. One duplicate runs towards Ian but gets flipped over the railing. Ian then takes his sword and begins to swing it, fighting the rest off. Dream Man notices that he doesn't have as many duplicates as before. Dream Man swoops in, grabs Ian by the back of the head, and slams his head to the wall. He repeatedly does this until he teleports Ian through the wall and into another wall. Ian elbows Dream man on his right rib, which causes him to let go of Ian.

Ian: That's all you got?

Dream Man: There is more of where that came from!

Dream Man teleports underneath Ian, grabbing him by the foot. Ian falls through and lands on the top of the roof. Dream Man then stomps onto Ian's chest, breaking him through the ceiling, and back down to the third floor.

Ian POV: (coughing up blood) Yeah, that wasn't fun. But him putting me through the roof left some sunlight through.

Dream Man: Get up! I'm not done with you!

Ian blocks a punch from Dream Man and then hits Dream man with a back elbow. Before Dream man can process this, Ian picks him up by his collar and tosses him back towards the ceiling.

BOOM!

The helicopter falls through the ceiling along with Dream Man, starting a fire in the building.

Will and the other employees are shaken up. Alisha wakes up and looks for Will.

Alisha: Uncle Will, she did it!

Dream Man duplicate: Who did what?

Alisha: Umm. Nothing! Nothing at all.

Dream Man duplicate: Tell me now!

Will grabs the duplicate and pushes him away.

Will: Stay away from her!

Duplicate: That's it!

The duplicate grabs an employee

The employee begins to scream. The duplicate raises his gun at her, but is saved by Ian. Ian cuts the duplicate in half with his sword.

Alisha: Dad!

Ian: Alisha. Are you okay?

Alisha and Ian hug.

Ian: Okay, everyone, we need to get out of here now, Will, lead these folks out of here. Dream Man's going to be here any minute, and I don't know where he will be coming fro-

Dream Man crashes through the wall and tackles Ian through another wall.

Will: Well, that's our cue; let's get out of here.

Alisha: We need to get Erin!

Will: I know where she's at!

Dream Man throws Ian onto the wall and knees him in his sternum.

Dream Man: That simple, huh? You thought I was done?

Ian: Not at all!

Ian headbutts Dream Man in the nose. Dream Man realizes something is off when Ian lands a hook on the left side of his jaw, and it feels like he knocks a tooth out. The Dream Man spits the tooth out.

Ian: Oh! Glass jaw, huh?

Dream Man: Lucky punch. Little stronger than imagined. Won't happen again.

Dream Man goes for a teleportation grab, but Ian counters it with a running spin heel kick to the right side of his ribs, which breaks them.

Dream Man: (spits out blood) Oh Nah! Something's not right! How are you doing this?

Ian: Maybe I'm just better! Faster and stronger!

Dream Man: (Thinking) Where's that time traveler at?

Dream Man throws a wall at Ian, knocking Ian unconscious. He then teleports to all the empty rooms. He sees Will and Alisha going into the room that Erin's in.

Will: Erin! Wake up! Time to wake up.

Erin wakes up and hugs Will. Dream Man teleports into the room.

Dream Man: You guys are clever. How far back did you go, Erin?

Erin: (smiling) Enough to learn a little bit more about you! And enough to take some powers away!

Dream Man: NO! No! No! This will not end like this! I'm going to win! I need to win!

Alisha: You can't! You won't! You don't even have all your powers anymore!

Erin: Yeah! And I know everything about you. I know all your little secrets too. And I know that you don't even like pizza!

Alisha: How dare you not like pizza!

Dream Man: (smirking) This is unbelievable. You two are much more than what I would've given you credit for. I gave Ian an offer a very long time ago, when he was as young as you two.

Alisha: We know! But you tried to trick him! And he saw right through you!

Dream Man: Yeah, but what he didn't tell you is that I really wanted him on my team at first. I thought he was going to be the best ally I would've had.

Will: Don't believe him, girls, these lies that he keeps telling!

Dream Man: I truly did want him. But I saw the danger he could be, like I've seen in others. His potential might be more harmful to us all. Ian is completely unique; he literally holds a star inside of him. He has the power of the sun flowing through him. That will be more dangerous than I ever will be! But you girls can actually do some good. Come with me, and let's change and shape the world how we would like it. Alisha, you weren't able to see past your death, but look, you are passed that now. Sleep again, and you will see our future ruling things. And you, Erin, we can continue back and help people. It's a lot you two will learn under my guidance.

Alisha: No! That will not work with us! You're scared that you're about to lose. You're now scared of life moving on without you! Not only that, but you fear pain and scared to die! You can feel it, can't you? You see it now! Defeat!

Dream Man teleports towards them, knocking Will away. Dream man grabs Alisha and Erin.

Dream Man: Gotcha! I tried to give you two one last chance! And you made the same mistake Ian did!

Alisha: (Gasping for air) You. You said that you needed the machine to get our powers!

Dream Man: I do, but I'll take my chances now. I've been patient long enough. You all have destroyed my machines, my building is burning down, and I have lost some powers! Well, no more! No more waiting.

Erin tries to lift her arms up towards Dream Man.

Dream Man: Oh no, little Erin!

Dream Man grabs Erin by her wrists and picks her up.

Erin: Let me Go! Let me Go!

Dream Man: Nah! I want you to watch what happens to your sister! This is what you will experience here in a moment, Erin! (Turning to Alisha) This might sting a little, little Miss Sunshine!

Just as Dream Man's about to take Alisha's powers, Ian comes flying in, kicking Dream Man in the back.

Dream Man: Ahhh! (Dream man drops the girls. He goes flying out of the room)

Ian: Sunshine, huh? You got a lot of nerve calling her that! Alisha, get your sister, get your uncle, and get out of here. I'm finishing this!

Alisha: (Coughing, catching her breath) Dad, this place is coming down! You need to come wit-

Ian: (staring at Dream Man) I'll be okay. Do as I ask.

Will: You heard the man Alisha, we need to go now!

Dream Man: Still trying to convince yourself you can win. I must say, though, that kick really did hurt. That idea of yours worked. Well, Erin's part of the plan worked somewhat.

Ian: You still don't see it, do you? Did you think our plan was just taking your powers? This place is burning down. Your facility is burning down!

Dream Man: So? I'll build a new one. I know a brilliant architect.

Ian: Hmm! How will you do any of that? If you're still asleep? This isn't even you, is it? This is a duplicate of yourself, right? The real you is still sleeping, dreaming, burning in another room. You might want to get there before it's too late!

Dream Man is speechless. The side of the face begins to sweat and burn. He tries to jump back into his body, but can't.

Ian: Can't get back there, can you? Little E is a lot more powerful than we both imagined. I see why you would want her powers.

Dream Man: What is she doing? Why can't I revert to my body?

Ian: She's blocking you. She has separated you from your actual body. These are some smart girls. And she's they're gone. Feel a little weaker, huh? Not so powerful. Just how it should be. Evenly matched!

Dream Man: This can't be happening. I should've killed you a long time ago!

Ian: Funny, isn't it? You are taking and killing others, children in their dreams, robbing them of life. All for you to be burned in a dream yourself. Poetic, actually.

Dream Man: You've robbed me! You've taken what isn't yours! Give it back, give it all back now!

Ian: I'll give you this in return.

Ian runs towards Dream man. Dream Man teleports behind Ian and goes to grab Ian's shoulder, but Ian elbows Dream Man. Ian grabs Dream Man and rams him into the wall. Ian punches Dream Man in the face, but Dream Man quickly counters with a knife stab into Ian's left side.

Ian is about to slam Dream man's head again, but is met with a kick push to another room. Dream Man kicks Ian onto his feet, then punches Ian through a wall.

Dream Man: C'mon, hero. Get up! Contest for your daughter! Fight for your "truth."

Dream Man slides out his sword and swings at Ian. Ian rolls over and pulls his sword out, blocking Dream Man's attack. Ian quickly gets to his feet, and he's met with another swing from Dream Man.

Dream Man: (grunting, mumbling) You take from me! You think you've won!

Ian POV: I got him losing control now. He's getting desperate. I need to find another opening to hit him by surprise.

Dream Man swings his sword wildly, leaving his right side open. Ian notices. Dream Man goes for a backhand swing with his right; Ian dodges back but immediately charges in with his sword and cuts the inside of Dream Man's right arm, cutting a vein.

Dream Man: (Drops his sword and goes down to a knee holding his arm) Ahhh!

Ian: Give up!

Dream Man: (continues to sweat and has his face burning. The left side of him catches fire.) Yeah! We're near the end, aren't we? This is it, Ian. You win!

Ian, thinking, moves closer to Dream Man, still having his sword drawn toward Dream Man.

Ian: I've waited a long time to hear that! But I need you to say, you surrender!

Dream Man: (Head down) Sure, if that's what you want to hear. But I will never surrender to YOU!

Dream Man quickly slides his dagger out to his right hand, pushes Ian's sword out of the way with his left hand, and stabs Ian in the stomach.

Ian: Uh!

Dream Man:(Smiling) So long, Hero!

Dream Man tosses Ian over the balcony into the fire.

Alisha and Erin look up from the first floor as they leave the building.

Alisha: Daddy!

Erin: What happened, Alisha? What happened? Did something happen to Ian?

Dream Man looks at the girls and smiles.

Alisha: Nothing. Um. Just keep concentrating. My Dad is still trying to hold him off. We need to stay outside, too. This place is coming down.

Dream Man jumps down to the first floor, over the fire. He tries to run toward Alisha and Erin, but drops to his knees again because of his body still in flames.

Dream Man: Uhh! It hurts!

Alisha: Erin. How much power did you give me?

Erin: Some super strength, not much. Why? Is something wrong?

Alisha: Uh, yeah. Dream Man's coming our way now.

Will: Stand behind me! Where's Ian.

Alisha: He fell in the fire. I can try to hold him off now. Erin, just try keeping those powers of his blocked.

Erin: I'm trying. He's very strong, though.

Dream Man: Daddy's gone. I'm tired of being patient! My body is burning, and I don't have much time now!

Dream Man gets back on his feet, and dashes towards them. Knocking Will back, and grabs hold of Alisha and Erin's necks with his hands.

Alisha: Let! Let go of us!

Erin: Let us go!

Alisha and Erin are hitting, clawing, and scratching for Dream Man to drop them. But to no success, they begin to fade.

Dream Man: Yes! It will all be over here soon. It's okay.

Alisha fading, no fight left in her; she turns and looks at Erin. Erin has tears rolling down, and Alisha begins to cry too. She looks at Dream

Man, who is staring into the Sun, and the flames begin to dry off of him. But then she sees a glowing, fiery figure walking out of the burning facility. She sees Ian. She can hear the gasp of people in awe as he walks by. As Ian gets closer, Alisha smiles.

Dream Man: That's right, "Sunshine" smile. Everything will be O- Ugh.

Dream Man's eyes get wide, and he drops the girls. Looks down and sees he's been impaled through his back. He falls face first. Bleeding out with his eyes open, he sees Ian. Ian kneels down to Dream Man.

Ian: Doesn't feel so good, huh? Dying.

Dream Man: H...How? You were dead!

Ian: I don't know how, and I don't care at the moment. I will watch you die, just like you watched all these kids die for years. Just like my girls were dying moments ago. Just like you wanted me, too.

Dream Man: Please.

Ian: No! How does it feel? To know that, no one will help you. That last bit of hope that you just might make it will be gone.

Dream Man: I'm suffering. Please. Just end me. It hurts.

Ian watches. He makes no sound. Erin walks up beside him.

Erin: Remember?

Ian: Yeah, I remember.

Ian leaps and jumps back into the burning facility.

Alisha: Dad? Erin, what is he doing?

Erin: He's keeping his promise; he won't be a hypofit.

Alisha: What? What promise?

Ian jumps back out, holding Dream Man's body. He drops the body. Dream Man is still breathing, but is heavily burned.

Alisha: How is he not dead? And what's going on?

Ian: I'm keeping my promise. We need him alive.

CHAPTER 14

Promise Is What's Next

Will: What?

Alisha: Daddy? What? Keep him alive? He's dangerous!

Ian: I know. But he's going to be useful, especially when Mr. Zip gets his hands on him.

Erin: And? You also promised me?

Ian: Yes, and I promised Erin could keep him imprisoned until we get all of those powers out of him.

Alisha: And what happens when he wakes up and does the same thing? His most useful and strongest power are the dreams!

Ian: I know that, Alisha.

Alisha: So why make this decision? Is death not good enough for him?

Ian: Yes, it would be. Death would be an escape for him from all his past crimes. Justice needs to be served.

Will: This guy is far too dangerous to keep alive, Ian.

Ian: He also killed Brian. Erin's father. Your brother. She wants to hold him accountable for that. She has a special cell for him. Where? I do not know. I really don't want to know and couldn't care less. She might leave him in the Stone Ages or in a futuristic prison. I just support her decision. Make sure you tell your mom, though.

Will: This is a lot for a girl her age.

Ian: She's stronger than both of us, in all categories. You can try to stop her, but you're on your own.

Ian's glow simmers down as the sunsets.

Will: Will you be okay when the sun goes down? You were stabbed quite a bit there.

Ian: I'm not sure? I feel fine. But I've never been in a battle like that before.

Alisha: We won, Dad. Can you believe that? We won!

Ian: I know, my love.

Will: So now what? We all gotta go home. Numerous coworkers are dead.

Ian: I got a guy coming. He will clean all this up. He will know what to do. Go be with your colleagues, Will; let them know all is good and that they're safe now. Help is on the way. (To Alisha) Your mom… I'm sure she is worried, sick, and devastated over Brian. Alisha, comfort her and Erin as much as you can. They will need it.

Alisha: Yes, sir.

Ian: Little E, excellent job today. You know, for a seven-year-old, you are tough.

Erin: Thanks, Big I.

Ian hugs Alisha and Erin.

Ian: You two make the perfect team. One of a kind, in fact. The perfect duo. I'm proud of you both, and we wouldn't have succeeded without your hard work.

Will's cell phone rings.

Will: Hello, Nicole? Um yeah, sure. Who do you want to talk to?

Ian Walks away, watching the sunset end.

Alisha: Can I talk with her?

Will: Hold, hold on, Nicole. Here's Alisha right here.

Will hands Alisha the phone.

Alisha: Hello, Mom!

Nicole: Alisha? Oh my Goodness, are you two okay? My babies. Are you both still here?

Alisha: Yes, Mom. We did it. We beat him. Are you ok?

Nicole: (crying) I will be, but not until I see my babies!

Alisha: (crying) We've missed you. Erin has been so strong too, Mom!

Nicole: Put her on the phone, please!

Erin: Hello? Mommy?

Nicole: Hi, baby. Are you ok?

Erin: Yes, I am. I'm going to miss Daddy.

Nicole: Me too, honey! But he was strong and protected me. Just like Ian protected you two. Can you put Ian on the phone, please, baby?

Erin: Yes, ma'am.

They go out to get Ian. But something is not right. As Ian's glow is finally worn down, he begins another glow, and his skin starts moistures.

Erin: Mr. I!

Alisha: Daddy! Are you okay?

Ian begins to evaporate.

Ian: Stand back! I don't know what is going on with me... I don't want to hurt you girls. Everything will be okay. Protect your mom, and protect each other!

Ian evaporates into the air. Alisha and Erin, standing there confused.

Alisha: What just happened? Daddy?

Erin with her head down.

Erin: He's gone...

Alisha: Don't say that! He will be back. He's just resting in the sun or something... but he's not gone. He can't be... We just won.

Erin: He's gone, Alisha, he's gone.

Tears run down Alisha's face.

Alisha: Daddy...

Alisha and Erin hug and hold each other for comfort.

Nicole: What's going on? What happened?

Alisha: He's gone, mom. He just left!

Nicole: We are almost there. I. I think I see you!

Abruptly, the helicopter lands. Out steps, Mr. Zip.

Mr. Zip: Hi, you must be Alisha, and you must be Erin. Am I right?

Alisha: Yeah, who are you?

Mr. Zip: I'm your father's boss, Mr. Zip. Your father called and asked if I could take you all home. Where is Ian, by the way?

Alisha: He just evaporated in thin air. We don't know where he went.

Mr. Zip: Really? He always feared that would happen. These powers are very unpredictable. Well, I owe your father a debt. He saved my life about fifteen years ago...

Alisha: We know the story! Can you take us home now, please?

Mr. Zip: Well, we got business to tend to first, but you girls should get into the chopper with your mom.

Nicole: Mr. Zip?

Mr. Zip: We are coming, Nicole. Hold on. (turning back to the girls) Now when you girls get in there, don't tell your mom that Dream Man is alive. She'll freak out.

Alisha: Wait, how would you know he's alive?

Mr. Zip: I have a lot of faith in your father. I knew he would beat him. And I have a lot of faith in you girls. My debt is still unpaid to him. So, Alisha and Erin. Welcome to Zipcodes. You two will be trained by the best, just like Ian.

Alisha: What?

Mr. Zip: You girls will even get a special briefcase like him too. Cool right?

Erin: Yes! We'll be ninjas.

Alisha: Why? We're kids.

Mr. Zip: Powerful with great potential. Time to get to work! Now go on with your mama before she kills me for keeping you two away for so long!

Alisha and Erin run toward the helicopter and hug Nicole. Mr. Zip turns to the employees of DOP

Mr. Zip: Attention! Hello there! My name is Mr. Zip, and I'm the owner of Zipcodes delivery company. I know this is a very traumatizing and heartbreaking day. But you all will get through this, and I will make sure of this together. We will honor your fallen peers, and I will personally pay for damages, bills, and whatever the case may be to help you get your lives and the lives of your peer's families back together. I apologize for what you have lost because of this Man. But together, we will build collectively and be stronger. You don't have to answer today, but when you're ready and if you'd like, you all have a job working at Zipcodes, my science department. We can use great minds like yourselves, and I have the resources and money to ensure you are all taken care of.

The DOP employees clap and thank Mr. Zip.

Mr. Zip: No need to thank me, let's just get you all home, and get you to your families. As for the Dream Man, he's coming too. Justice will be served, so let's get him gets him on my plane too. Seems like he'll be out for a while.

Elsewhere, Ian is awakened by rainy clouds. He goes to take shelter but is very unbalanced. He then sees a lonely scavenger.

Ian: Excuse me. Where am I?

The scavenger scans his face and sees him as an unknown species. He smiles. Ian tries to land a right hook but is met with a stunning sword to the arm. It knocks him out. He is then dragged through this cloudy town. He wakes up in a holding cell.)

Ian: (Waking up) This must be a mistake. I don't even know where I am. Why am I being held against my will? No rights read to me or anything. This is a lawsuit waiting to happen.

Cellmate: (loud laugh) You think you're still on Earth, huh?

Ian: What do you mean, "still think?"

Cell Mate: Take a look outside, man.

(Ian looks outside and sees a frozen moon orbiting them.)

Ian: Why is the moon frozen? And why is it bigger than what I remember?

Cell Mate: That's not a moon. That's the sun!

Printed in the United States
by Baker & Taylor Publisher Services